Watch a
Best wishes,
Jeannie Wycherley
x x x

THE MYSTERY OF THE MARSH MALAISE

WONKY INN BOOK 5

JEANNIE WYCHERLEY

The Mystery of the Marsh Malaise
Wonky Inn Book 5
by
JEANNIE WYCHERLEY
Copyright © 2019 Jeannie Wycherley
Bark at the Moon Books
All rights reserved

Sign up for Jeannie's newsletter: here
The Mystery of the Marsh Malaise was edited by Anna Bloom @
The Indie Hub
Cover design by Tammy.
Formatting by Tammy

Author's Note

This book, as with the whole of the Wonky Inn series, is set in East Devon in the UK.

It uses British English spellings, idioms and vernacular.

This book is dedicated to the real Ross Baines
remembering a 'perfect day'

CONTENTS

CHAPTER ONE

L ondon in the spring.

Gritty drops of rain spattered against my skin, the backdrop of the day relentlessly grey. People, people everywhere, rushing to get where they needed to be. I stalked purposefully along beside a busy road, wondering whether all Londoners are permanently late for meetings and appointments. Do they think that if they move quickly enough they will fit more activity into their day? Is everything timetabled? Every coffee break, every trip to Selfridges or a cinema complex, every stroll in the park—slotted between the cramped narrow lines in a bulging well-thumbed diary, or digitally recorded on a mobile phone?

I paused outside an innocuous-seeming bookshop on Charing Cross Road. My heart beat a little too fast as a London bus trundled by, alarmed as always by any unexpected flash of red. Whittle-combe and the peace of Devon's beautiful country-side seemed a million miles away. Here the speed of movement, the metallic and chemical scent of fumes that perfumed the air, the noise of traffic and the cooing of pigeons, the sheer dull grimness of the historic facades, overloaded my senses and induced feelings of anxiety.

As if I wasn't anxious enough.

I'd been accustomed to the pace of city life once, not that long ago really, but now everything had changed. The threat was real.

I rushed through the door of the bookshop into the labyrinth of shelves beyond, pushing it closed behind me, shutting out most of the sound. In here the noise was muted by the millions and millions of paper pages. Volumes that soaked up volume. The sudden calm provided relief to my jangling nerves.

I quickly made my way to the very back of the shop, through the children's section, and took the half dozen steps down into a lower floor. No windows here, just artificial lighting. Fluorescent batons that flickered and buzzed. At the very back of the shop, in the dead zone, the shelves held dozens and dozens of shabby second-hand tomes relating to early-modern and modern engineering, the growth of the UK canal network, and a history of road surfaces.

Not an overly popular section.

I placed my hand against a particularly weighty volume, the gilt lettering so faded it was impossible to read the title, and pushed hard. The shelves fell away from me. Glancing quickly behind me to ensure the coast was clear, I skipped through, and returned the secret door to its original position, pausing long enough to hear the reassuring click as it closed securely.

I followed a narrow corridor, the pea-green walls scuffed and dirty, the lighting muted, down another few steps, through another couple of anonymous doors until I found the exit. A light above the door glowed—a bright forbidding red. A state-of-the-art security system had been installed here recently, and now a camera traced all movement. I pressed the screen to the side of the door, allowing some computer somewhere to read the lines on my palm before deciding whether to allow me access or not.

A buzz. A click. The light above the door flicked to green.

I made my way into Celestial Street.

This time however I had no meeting scheduled with Penelope Quigwell, no arrangement with

Wizard Shadowmender to catch up for a cosy chat, a pie and a pint in *The Half Moon Inn*. Instead, I ensured my cloak was pulled up to cover my face and turned into the drizzle, walking quickly along the darker side of the road. I ignored the brightly lit and welcoming shops, turning right into a narrow passageway known as Cross Lane instead. The space between houses here grew ever narrower, maybe eight to ten feet at its widest. At this end, closest to the shops, you could find seamstresses and tailors, the odd carpenter and cobbler. This was as far as most people ventured.

As I progressed further along the narrow lane the houses bowed out towards me. It became increasingly difficult to pass another person without turning sideways on. Front doors opened onto front doors, and the opening between houses let only a splinter of daylight through. In places, the only illumination spilt from the windows of the ramshackle dwellings. Occasionally I passed such a window, lit by a candle, and glancing inside would spot a fire burning. Some of the little front parlours presented themselves as cosy and snug, but many others were dank and miserable. For the most part I averted my eyes, certain there were things happening behind these doors that I did not need to know about.

There were name plaques displayed on many of the doors here, shadowy businesses, people who kept to themselves and guarded their secrets closely. Other travellers along this narrow pathway—and there were a surprising number of them—turned their faces away from the light and from curious gazes or indolent stares. The deeper into Cross Lane you ventured, the more likely you were to be desirous of avoiding scrutiny.

My mother Yasmin had warned me repeatedly as a small child never to stray into Cross Lane. Later, after my father had disappeared and my mother had become reclusive and angry, she'd granted me more independence. Or perhaps I had stolen it away, conveniently capitalizing on her grief as she withdrew. My own anger towards her seemed selfish and out of place now. Still, she had mentioned many times that Cross Lane was not a fitting place for a good and decent witch to be found.

But perhaps the time had come for me to relinquish any hold I had on the notion that I was good and decent.

Maybe I didn't want to be any more.

Just as the tiny alley narrowed even further and a few feet above my head the houses on either side practically touched, thereby robbing the lane completely of natural light while sheltering me from the rain, the row of houses came to an abrupt end. I stumbled into a kind of courtyard that formed a crossroads. I had never travelled this far along Cross Lane before. I peered tentatively around. Small black signs with gold letters pointed left and right, back the way I'd come and onwards... to who-knew-where. My instructions had been to take the first left, down Knick-Knack Lane.

I followed the directions given, passing more people than I'd imagined I'd see down here. No doubt about it, I was among the underbelly of my kind. These were folk who had existed on the periphery of the circles in which I'd moved my entire life. My mother and her ilk—the coven to which we belonged headed of course by Wizard Shadow-mender—were all above board and decent. We prac-tised magick as part of the mundane societies in which we moved, surreptitious and private when it came to what we did.

Here, in the backwaters behind Celestial Street, these were darker, marginalized witches, wizards, mages and sages, sorcerers and sorceresses.

Fifty yards along Knick-Knack Lane I spotted an iron sign swinging in a slight breeze from the second storey of an Elizabethan Inn. *The Web and Flame.*

My destination.

The Web and Flame was everything *The Half Moon Inn* was not. A proper old-fashioned spit-and-sawdust pub, with roughly hewn benches and worn wooden tables. The rooms were small and dimly lit. They could have been cosy with the right décor, maybe a smattering of candles in coloured jars and a few scattered cushions and pictures here or there. But the walls were whitewashed and the fires burned without cheer.

A toothless and bald man in his late fifties, wearing a hessian sack as a bar apron, regarded me through hooded eyes, his expression vaguely hostile.

"Good afternoon," I said, standing tall, attempting to exude a confidence I didn't truly possess.

"What can I get you?" he asked.

I scanned the ales on display and opted for a glass of *Hoodwinker*. When he poured it the colour was dark and rich, so I expected it to taste bitter, and yet when I took a mouthful I found it to be light and fresh, citrusy. A hoodwinker indeed.

The bartender took my money then nodded at a table behind me. I turned.

The pub was largely empty and the few people inhabiting the tables stared disconsolately into the bottom of their pint glasses and tankards, minding their own business. Only one man looked my way.

I walked towards him, self-conscious under his gaze, my stomach fluttering. I paused at his table and placed my hand on the wooden chair facing him.

"Is this seat taken?" I asked.

He was a wizard, a man in his mid-thirties perhaps, handsome, with dark hair that curled around his collar and equally dark eyes that glittered at me with unconcealed interest.

"That depends." He cocked his head and waited.

I experienced a moment of uncertainty. I'd been playing out this meeting in my mind for over a week, and now here I stood, and I could feel my resolve slipping. Had I found the right man or not? I had an envelope full of money burning a hole in a hidden pocket in my cloak. The last thing I wanted to do was to hand it over to someone completely unworthy.

We locked gazes. I could see amusement in his eyes, but also a steely determination. He wasn't someone who would suffer fools.

That made my mind up. I hoisted the heavy envelope from my pocket and lay it on the table in front of him. He watched me do so, and smirked. I kept my fingers pressed against the envelope, driving my weight down through them, impaling the money safely into place. "*Viscus in loco.*"

He laughed and sprawled back against the wall.

"Do sit down, Ms Daemonne," he said, keeping his voice low. "You're making the place look untidy."

I pulled the chair out and as I did so, quick as a flash he reached out. Tapping the envelope once he scooped it up easily enough, palming it so that it disappeared up his sleeve.

I settled myself in the chair, smiling. "I seem to have found the right place."

"This is only half of what we agreed," the man said, patting the side of his jacket.

He was good. "I know. You get the other half when you join me at Whittle Inn."

The man mock-pouted. It didn't suit him. "You don't trust me." A statement not a question.

"Of course not." I folded my arms and studied his features carefully. Tanned skin, full lips, a little dimple in his chin, wrinkles around eyes framed by the most amazing eyelashes, long and black. He liked to smile.

"That's good to hear." He regarded me a little longer before leaning across the table, close enough that I could have kissed him had I so desired. I felt his breath on my face. "You wear your heart on your sleeve."

I nodded, pressing my lips together.

"Your magick is weak." He tapped his side again where the money was now safely stowed.

"If it was stronger then I wouldn't need you," I retorted, my words laden with ice.

"Why should I help you?"

I widened my eyes in surprise. He was a gun for hire. "Because I'm paying you handsomely to do so."

He gave a slight head shake. "I don't need your money."

"You quite clearly do." I couldn't help but contradict him. His clothes were good quality but well worn. If he had any wealth at all I wouldn't have found him here in Knick-Knack Lane. He'd have been lording it somewhere less inauspicious and disreputable.

His eyes glittered with a flash of annoyance. He had pride. Interesting.

"Is money all that matters to you?"

"No, of course not," I protested. *Not at all. That's why I'm risking a lot of it throwing it away on someone like you.*

"Then don't presume to judge me by those standards, Ms Daemonne."

I cast a quick look over my shoulder. Everyone appeared to be keeping their own counsel, but you could never tell. I didn't like that he kept using my name.

"You're a fool if you think no-one will know you've been here," he said quietly.

"I'm desperate."

He flung his head back and roared with laughter. "Obviously. Otherwise you wouldn't be seen with me. I should be insulted."

Should I apologise that I'd hurt his feelings? I didn't have time for this. I rubbed my eyes wearily. He watched me do so and reached out to take my hand. I tried to snatch it away, but he pulled it towards himself, turning it over so that it was palm up, and read what he saw there.

When he looked up again, his face had softened.

"I can't help you," he said. "You're in too deep."

"Then give me my money back," I demanded, gritting my teeth in annoyance.

A sharp shake of the head. "I can't do that."

"Then you should be a man of your word and abide by the contract implicitly accepted when you took the envelope."

He grinned, but without humour. "If you wanted

an honourable man you would be undertaking your business in *The Half Moon Inn*."

I pushed my chair back in annoyance and rose.

"If *you* were everything you claimed to be you'd be sitting on the Council of Witches," I retorted, and whirled away in fury. I marched out of the pub, not caring who watched my sulky exit.

I'd made it almost as far as the crossroads when I heard feet running after me. Instinctively, imagining it to be a thief, I turned to ward off a blow, but it was only my dark-haired acquaintance. He reached out to grab my arm, and when I tried to pull away, still angry with him, he fell into step beside me.

"You're beautiful when you're angry."

"Take your hand off me. I'm not interested." I pushed him away and strode into Cross Lane where it was too narrow for him to walk with me. He followed on behind.

"You want to know whether he's still alive, don't you?"

I froze, then slowly swung to face him, dreading to see mockery in his eyes.

His face looked deadly serious, grim almost.

"Is he?"

He stepped towards me, his black eyes boring into mine. "He's a mortal, you know? Expendable."

I lifted my left hand—where my engagement ring, a large black stone set between two diamonds sparkled with life in the subdued light—and placed it on the necromancer's chest.

"He means the world to me. Now tell me whether he's alive."

CHAPTER TWO

"I sense thunder in your heart, Alf." Wizard Shadowmender strolled beside me as we wandered through Speckled Wood. Ostensibly we were inspecting the boundaries that formed the bulk of Whittle estates. Speckled Wood gently transitioned into forest land here, the forest that stretched north and east towards the hills, with Abbotts Cromleigh lying to the north-west.

"You don't have to be a wizard to know that." I kept my tone light, but even so the curt response hit home and proved his point. I winced inwardly.

He took my arm. "Come, come my dear. I hate to see you like this."

"Has there been any word?" I knew what the answer would be. I must have asked the same question of everyone I'd met who might have had any inkling at all. *Have you heard anything about George? Do you know where he is? Is he alive?*

I was a broken record.

"You know if there had been I would not have kept it from you. You would be the very first person I'd inform."

"Yes." I sighed. We'd entered a clearing, halting at the edge of a large pool of water, listening to the toads calling around us. The birds tweeted in the trees on the edges, totally unconcerned about us. About anything.

I pulled my arm away from Wizard Shadow-mender and, manoeuvring myself over the rocks, crouched by the pool. In this part of Speckled Wood the ground dipped in a large hollow and water collected here, fed in part by a series of freshwater springs that ran both overland and under the ground. In turn this pool, when it was full, spilled over to be consumed by the marshes. After a wet few months, both the pool and the marshes were swollen. Everywhere I looked the forest here teemed with life. Frogs and toads, and plenty of insects skating on the water, or alighting on the algae that formed as part of the natural bio-system. The birds were attracted to the area too, thanks to the sheer abundance of creepy crawlies that skittered around. Pond plants grew thigh high, sheltering and disguising predators of all kinds.

The long-range weather forecast for the summer seemed brighter, so I expected much of the marsh would dry out, but for now this had become my new favourite place to hang out. It brought me a certain level of peace.

"It's been seven weeks." I agitated the water with the tips of my fingers. Several watermen scattered away from me in alarm.

"And three days." Wizard Shadowmender joined me at the edge of the pool. He'd been counting as well then. "You are not alone in this, Alf. Never alone."

We were all in this together. That's what Wizard Shadowmender was trying to tell me, and yes, that made me feel somewhat better, but didn't alter the fact that The Mori seemed to have hit me disproportionately hard. They had tried—and fortunately failed—to take my inn and my land away, but they'd managed to stir up trouble and alienate some of the Whittlecombe villagers who were my tenants.

And they'd almost succeeded in killing me. If it hadn't been for the spirit water witches in Whittlecombe's village pond then I'd have been done for, that much was certain.

So, because they hadn't succeeded in finishing me off, they'd taken George from me. And I had no idea whether he was alive or dead, and seemingly, no way of ever finding out.

"I have eyes and ears everywhere, Alf. I have technical wizards scanning every known electronic frequency. We have reached out to all of our folk on the peripheries—even those we generally hold little truck with." He meant faeries and vampires.

I recognized how broad and deep Wizard Shadowmender's networks were. I knew he was doing his best. But I'd always been impatient and I desperately wanted to hear some news that would confirm George still lived.

I dipped my fingers into the water once more. Deliciously cool and clear. I could see tiddlers darting here and there among the reeds. It was shallow nearest to the bank, but rapidly became deeper. In the summer, if enough water remained, and the season turned out to be as hot as it had been when I'd first arrived in Whittlecombe, maybe I'd come out here and skinny dip. My guests from the inn tended not to venture this far into Speckled Wood, so it would be private enough.

"Any fresh sightings of our friends?" Wizard Shadowmender interrupted my thoughts.

"A few. I've been out most evenings. Finbarr and I have spotted one or two, but always from a distance. By the time we get anywhere close to them they've disappeared." Finbarr, a weasel-faced witch who claimed to be descended from a leprechaun, had turned into a good and faithful friend. He'd been staying with me at the behest of Wizard Shadowmender for the past few weeks. The little fella could be annoying, like a younger brother, but I was grateful for his presence. We were opposites. He was talkative when I was feeling morose, energetic at all the wrong times of the day, and curious about everything. He never stopped asking questions. When I grew tired of him and told him I needed to be alone, he would bother the ghosts or Charity.

Everybody loved him though. His eternally upbeat personality and sing-song accent were uplifting. And he'd been a complete boon to me. His magick had proved to be powerful, and he had grown adept at fixing the barrier that Mr Kephisto had weaved around the grounds and the inn to keep The Mori at bay.

I had never asked him to accompany me on my forays around Whittlecombe, but he always did. At these times he reined in his exuberance, proving himself as a watchful ally, and an acute observer instead. His senses were sharp. He never missed a trick.

"They must have a base around here," Wizard Shadowmender mused and I nodded in agreement.

"The most obvious place would be Piddlecombe Farm as I've told you before. That seems to be the locus of a great deal of activity."

"But you can't get close enough?"

"I daren't get closer." The place unnerved me. It seemed indisputable that Piddlecombe Farm was where I'd been held on the night I'd been abducted. And George had been calling me from there on the night he disappeared. The police had searched but found nothing. The farm had been deserted.

I swished my hand around in the pool, watching the water as it bubbled. I felt the tingle of something —akin to a gentle electric shock—and I stopped moving my hand and waited for the water to settle.

"If I thought we could get away with it, I'd send in a party of witches one night to investigate, but I'd be worried about an ambush. I need more intelligence first."

The water stilled, and I stared down at the silt, a foot or so below the surface. I waited.

"Alf?" Wizard Shadowmender prompted when I didn't immediately reply.

I removed my hand from the water. "Do you think there are eels in here?"

"Eels?" Wizard Shadowmender scanned the pool. "I shouldn't have thought so." He sounded doubtful. "The river doesn't flow into it, does it?"

"No. Just a few of the springs." I shook my hand, sprinkling sparkling drops of water over myself. They clung like crystals to my robes. "I suppose you're right. There wouldn't be eels in here." Were there any other kinds of fish that could give you a little shock? I dipped my hand in the water again and experienced the small tingle once more. *How odd.* More than likely it was simply due to the temperature of the water.

I stood, wiping my hands against my robes. Wizard Shadowmender looked perplexed. "Problem?"

"Probably not." I hooked my arm through his. "Ignore me."

"I would never do that, Alf. You're very important to me."

I smiled, with genuine pleasure. It touched me that he cared. And of course he was doing everything possible to help locate George. He would do no less than his best. I knew that.

"Let's go back to the inn," I said. "I expect

Monsieur Emietter has prepared lunch by now, and it's always a treat."

"Oh indeed it is," Wizard Shadowmender enthused, his cherubic cheeks flushing pink. "You certainly dine well at Whittle Inn."

When I have an appetite, I thought. Mine had gone AWOL over the past few weeks.

"As long as it isn't eel," I joked, glancing back at the still water behind me. The surface rippled and I frowned, but quickly dismissed the disturbance as a bird or an insect, and led the elderly wizard back into the wood, heading for home.

We ate in the kitchen, leaving the bar area for the guests. The inn was running at 80 percent capacity, so the ghosts were busy serving lunch and drinks. I'd even pulled Zephaniah and Ned in from the garden where they'd been working on a new vegetable patch out the back near the storage sheds. In my wisdom I'd decided that it would be fabulous if we were able to serve vegetables grown on our own grounds. Gwyn, my great grandmother, had been an enthusiastic proponent of this as she had once cultivated a herb garden herself, so I'd roped her in too.

I liked to keep her busy.

We'd had a large greenhouse installed and set aside a good-sized area for Ned and Zephaniah to try their hand at growing beans, peas, carrots and parsnips, onions and tomatoes. In the greenhouse we nurtured some salad leaves and more tomatoes, basil and parsley. In the herb patch, Gwyn, given free rein, was working wonders with sage, thyme, mint, rosemary and chives.

For now, Wizard Shadowmender and I dined on peppered mackerel, caught locally at Durscombe a few miles away, baby potatoes from Whittle Stores and a mixed summer salad. I picked at mine absently but tried to join in with the general conversation around me. Charity and Florence regaled the elderly wizard with a few funny stories of things found in the guest rooms.

"We could have a box full of wands, you know?" Charity told him. "We always contact the guest and ask if they would like their property returned and for the most part they take us up on that. I suppose a wand is a vital piece of equipment for many of you folk." She chewed on some fish. "They're all so different, aren't they? Wands?"

"Yes, to each their own." Shadowmender agreed.

"But some witches don't use one at all." He looked pointedly at me. I never did.

"Neither does Mr Kephisto," I pointed out. Mr Kephisto was my nearest neighbouring wizard, living just over the river in Abbotts Cromleigh.

"That's usually true. Although he does sometimes. Some witches can use anything. Household implements for example." Wizard Shadowmender brandished his knife and fork. "Cutlery."

"Really?" Charity looked on as Wizard Shadowmender sent the salt and pepper cellars scuttling across the table with a little burst of magick from the end of his fork. "A wand in and of itself is not magick. It just helps to direct your intent." He lay his fork down and beckoned the salt back with a quick kink of his index finger.

Charity laughed, as delighted as any child by the Wizard's display. "Clever!"

Florence, busily wiping down a worktop, called back over her shoulder. "I don't mind when we find wands. I'm less keen on some of the rubbish that gets left behind. Half-eaten sandwiches, apple cores and stuff like that. And heaven-to-Betsy, all the bird and rabbit bones and innards is a bit much."

"Yeah. What's that about?" Charity grimaced.

"Mr Hoo enjoys the leftover innards," I

remarked wryly. "It saves him having to go out and hunt at night." My feathered friend could be remarkably lazy at times.

"Well I know what to do with them from now on." Florence looked disapproving and Charity tittered, helping herself to a slice of bread and butter.

"We have quite a collection of items in our lost property box," she said. "Don't we Alf? We were keeping them in a cupboard under the stairs, but they outgrew that space and now we've set aside a section of the attic."

"What else has been left here?" Wizard Shadowmender asked, smiling at me, obviously noting my dejection.

"Brollies, books, including several spell books and journals, hats—" Charity offered.

"Underwear," Florence giggled.

"Single shoes and boots." Charity shook her head. "Why anyone forgets to pack both parts of a pair I have no idea."

"Spectacles, a wig—" I suggested.

"Jewellery. You name it," Florence finished.

"Why is it never claimed?" Wizard Shadowmender asked.

Charity shrugged. "Well, like I said, we try and

reunite goods with their owners, but sometimes they deny ownership, or we can't get in touch."

"And sometimes, given the nature of the guests we see here at Whittle Inn, I suppose they're simply being secretive," I offered.

I thought back to the mysterious Mr Wylie, a guest at the time of George's disappearance. I'd asked Florence to spy on him and all she could tell me was that he wasn't whom he claimed to be. Not a businessman as he'd previously told Charity, that much seemed clear. Enquiries via Wizard Shadowmender had led to naught.

I sighed. My head made constant loops, trying to make sense of all the recent goings on. We had more questions than answers and I hated it.

Wizard Shadowmender reached out and squeezed my hand. "Patience," he said, and his knowing eyes shone with intelligence and compassion, and filled me with strength.

I took a deep breath and smiled. "Yes," I answered simply.

After a cup of tea to finish our meal, I walked him to the front door of the inn to see him out. He shook hands with a few of the guests who were hanging out in the bar whom he knew, and then I waited as he exchanged a few words with Frau

Kirsch in excellent German. His skills never ceased to amaze me.

Finally he joined me, and I helped him into a waiting taxi.

"Back to Surbiton now?" I asked. Wizard Shadowmender lived in the most ordinary looking house, on the dullest estate I had ever seen. Grey pebbledash and an ugly garage made up the external view, but once inside you were transported to something more akin to an enchanted castle, all tapestry walls and huge log fire places.

"London first. Celestial Street," Shadowmender corrected me, then studied my face. "A little bird tells me that you were there last week."

I kept my face blank. *My, my. Word does get around.*

"Briefly," I said, meeting his gaze. He continued to stare at me, and I instinctively understood that he knew I'd taken a walk on the wild side. But I couldn't come clean. I obfuscated. "Just picking up some new robes." It was a lie. He would know it was a lie. But the words were out, and it was too late to take them back.

He nodded. "You didn't pop in to see Penelope?"

Penelope Quigwell he meant. My lawyer, and the woman in charge of overseeing the finances relating to the Whittle Estate. I shook my head. "No, not this time. It was a flying visit."

Wizard Shadowmender smiled. Not a hint of rancour in his expression. Instead he gave me a quick hug and settled down into the back of the car, nodding at his driver.

"If you need anything at all, just get in touch through the orb."

"I will."

"And stop worrying, Alf. Take care of yourself and your inn and everything else will fall into place."

"Okay. Will do." I tried to present a purposeful and positive façade.

With one more knowing glance, he waved, and the driver started the engine. I watched them disappear down the drive, wondering why he hadn't challenged me when he knew I'd been telling fibs.

A sudden shriek from the inn behind me startled me out of my reverie. I dashed back inside, expecting to find someone being murdered, only to witness half a dozen pixies running riot around the bar.

"Finbarr!" I bellowed. The goddess alone knew why Finbarr liked to invite his pixies out to play. I think he used them in his magick practice. This had been a regular occurrence since he'd moved into the inn. He only had to take his eyes off them for one moment and they played havoc, shrieking like banshees and running around the inn causing chaos, disrupting guests and creating a crazy mess.

"I'm coming, I'm coming," the little auburn-haired witch yelled from the top of the first flight of stairs. "Hey guys!" he shouted at the pixies and they sped away, through the rear door of the bar, into the back passage where The Snug and The Nook were located, and the kitchen beyond them. He threw himself down the stairs and ran after them. "Wait up. Wait up!"

"Finbarr," I scolded, "you'd better not let them get close to the kitchen or Monsieur Emietter will be scooping out your insides and creating Irish pâté."

"I'm on it! Don't you be worrying about that now."

I wished everyone would stop telling me not to worry.

I would worry if I wanted to.

The front gardens of the inn were looking lovely. I leaned out of my bedroom window examining the flower beds from the higher vantage point. Pansies and peonies of varying colours were exploding into life. The rose bushes were coming on, and there were beds of green that promised to turn into a summery explosion of sweet peas soon enough. Ned and Zephaniah had done an amazing job of turning what had been little more than a wasteland twelve months ago into a pretty escape, perfect for the guests to amble around, or play outdoor games when the weather was fine.

That reminded me. I intended to purchase some deck chairs so that people could sit out there when the summer arrived properly. It wouldn't be too long now.

This afternoon there was some definite warmth in the air, although the cloud was low, and the sun had yet to succeed in burning through it. I imagined we were finally going to have some decent weather.

Good. I was heartily fed up of the rain.

I leaned further out of the window to check on the wisteria bushes growing along this side of the inn.

"I can't see any evidence of new robes, Alfhild."

The sudden clipped tones of my great grand-mother, Gwyn, chimed loudly in my ear, startling me so that I almost lost my balance. I clutched at the windowsill in panic.

"Grandmama," I protested. "Do you mind? A

little warning please. I could have gone over the edge."

She stood with her arms folded, glowering at me. "Did you just lie to Wizard Shadowmender, Alfhild?"

"You know I did." I folded my own arms across my chest and mirrored her body language.

"Daemonnes don't lie."

"We do if we're pushed into a tight corner," I volleyed back at her. "And that's where I'm at right now."

"What did you go to London for?"

"I can't tell you."

"Was it to meet this Hortense chap?"

"Have you been reading my mail?" I asked crossly. Of course she had. Nothing in this inn was sacrosanct. It was like living in the MI5 headquarters, spies everywhere.

"I just happened to see a letter you'd left open on your desk."

"That's a likely story." I wagged my finger at her. "I don't leave letters open on my desk. You must have been snooping."

"I'm allowed to snoop. I'm your great grandmother. And I was here before you."

We glared at each other, until the ridiculousness

of the situation hit home, and I laughed. It felt good to suddenly release the tension, and I laughed far longer than I might otherwise have done.

Gwyn relaxed and smiled too. "So tell me," she said, when I'd finished wiping tears of mirth from my eyes.

"His name is not Hortense, Grandmama, that's a girl's name."

She waved a hand at me. *Get on with it.* "Whatever," she said, mimicking the phrase Charity and I were forever coining.

"It's Horace T Silvanus. He likes to be known as Silvan."

Gwyn nodded. "If my name was Horace I'd want to be called something else too. What does the T stand for?"

"I have no idea. I didn't ask him."

"So you went to London to meet him? Is he your new love interest?"

"Grandmama!" I couldn't believe her sometimes.

"It's been a few weeks."

I goggled at her in exasperation. "I haven't given up on George yet! I never will. I'm going to find him."

A dubious expression crossed Gwyn's face. "Hmm."

"Don't you think I can?" I asked, and Gwyn shrugged. It concerned me that no-one else felt the passing of time the way I did. It was imperative to move quickly but only I seemed to want to do that. But then I suppose everyone else, like Wizard Shadowmender, was biding their time and waiting for a clue that would lead us to George.

They seemed to think we'd find George and rescue him, and everything would be fine. In my mind, I figured I'd have to fight a battle with The Mori first.

Hence the meeting with Silvan.

"I've invited Silvan here."

"To do what?" Gwyn asked, eyeing me with suspicion.

"To help me find George."

"Is he a detective?"

"No, nothing like that."

"What then?"

I shook my head, declining to answer, and headed for the open door and my study on the other side. "You'll find out if he comes."

"Well that doesn't sound very promising." Gwyn followed me and I tried to wave her away. "Is he coming or not?"

I frowned. I didn't know for sure. "He wouldn't

give me a straight answer."

"Pfft!" The look on Gwyn's face was a picture. An odd mix of triumph and despair. "What are you getting yourself into now, Alfhild?"

I threw myself into the seat behind my laptop and started hitting the keys with ferocity, entering and re-entering my password incorrectly.

I don't know, I wanted to cry. *I don't know, and no-one seems to want to help me. So I've taken the law into my own hands and I'm going to find George. Whatever it takes.*

But I didn't say that. I calmed my fingers and entered my password correctly, then looked up and smiled as benignly as I could manage. "I have to work, darling grandmama. I'm sure you understand."

We stared at each other for a long moment, until finally she nodded. "Very well," she said quietly, before slowly beginning to apparate.

As she disappeared, she couldn't resist a parting shot. "By the way, Alfhild, I went through your entire wardrobe and you do desperately need new robes. Perhaps you should go back up to London, and after you've finished shopping, find Wizard Shadow-mender and tell him all about Hortense."

"Not going to happen," I muttered under my breath, but she'd gone.

CHAPTER THREE

"Again," Silvan instructed.

Exhausted and dripping with sweat I directed a ball of energy at an empty whisky bottle. It skittered sideways. Silvan twitched his long thin black wand at it and it resumed its place with a shudder. We had taken refuge in the attic, practicing spells of force. We'd been at it for hours.

My spellcasting ability was weak. I'd vastly improved over the past twelve months, for sure, but even so, the years I'd spent hiding from my vocation had taken a toll. And that was why I'd visited the dark web, looking for someone to teach me all I needed to know. Or all I thought I needed to know. Through my enquiries I'd made some dubious contacts. Silvan was the result of my research.

Horace T Silvanus was a dark witch. A man who knew how to cast spells that hurt others. A being who could be totally devoid of compassion. A witch who could kill using his magick without thinking twice. He was a necromancer, meaning he could call on the dead and speak to them and enlist their help if he needed to.

But most of all he was a mercenary. A witch for hire. If I paid him enough, he'd do as I asked.

He encapsulated everything I understood a war witch to be. Shady, manipulative, merciless, deadly. And as far as I was concerned, we were at war.

With The Mori.

I'd realised after George's disappearance and the run-in we'd had with The Mori at the Fayre that I needed to upgrade my skills. Being 'nice Alf' simply wasn't going to cut it anymore.

Nice Alf wasn't going to bring George back.

Nasty Alf stood a chance.

This afternoon Silvan had me attempting to push back against the magick he used. To say I found myself struggling was an understatement. Moving objects is pretty much Spellcasting 101. So is blocking, or using a defence spell, when someone else throws or directs an object at you. Moving objects that someone else has control of, well that's a whole different ball game.

I'd tired rapidly. Working with Silvan took so

much out of me physically. I had muscles aching, especially in my shoulders, upper back and thighs, that I'd forgotten I had.

Silvan flicked his wand at the bottle again and it hurtled towards me. Instinctively I ducked rather than repel the bottle with my magick, and Silvan had to fling out a hand to catch it by its neck before it smashed into the wall behind me.

"Ugh," I cringed. After hours of practice, I just wasn't getting it. I slumped down over my knees, panting.

Silvan laughed. "Are you sure you want to go ahead with this? Perhaps you aren't fit enough."

Too much cake and not enough exercise. I stood, breathing hard, trying to bring my gasping under control. "I'm fine. Perfectly fine."

Silvan's eyes twinkled. "You have a very attractive flush." He indicated his own face. Not a bead of sweat to be seen. I knew I must look a state, all wild hair and red face.

"Let's try again," I said, struggling to catch my breath.

Florence picked that moment to glide into the room followed by a tray of sandwiches, cakes, fruit and a jug of water with two glasses. She looked at Silvan with wide eyes and he offered her a leering grin in return. If it's possible for a ghost to blush, I swear Florence did just that.

"Hi Florence," I said, attempting to distract her.

"Oh, Miss Alf," she smiled. "Sorry to interrupt you but we missed you at lunch and Charity thought you might be hungry."

Silvan examined the tray. "Leave the fruit and water and take the rest back," he said.

"But—" Florence glanced at me for confirmation.

"Go, go, go." He said, indicating the door with his wand.

Florence decanted the water, glasses and plate of fruit onto a side table and reluctantly took her leave, as I nodded my thanks.

Silvan tossed the empty whisky bottle he'd been clutching into the air, then guided it gently down to the floor. "We should try something else." He plucked a couple of bananas from the plate and threw one at me. I caught it.

"I was hungry enough for a sandwich," I said.

He moved over to stand next to me and tapped his wand against my stomach. "You've seen too many lunches. We need you to be fit and wiry. Fast-moving. Strong."

"Do we really?" I growled. I'd been thinking the same, but I didn't feel it was his place to articulate that thought. "I'm plenty fit enough." The goddess knew I should be, with the amount of running around after my guests and ghosts I did.

"You should channel that anger of yours into your magick," Silvan observed with a wry half-smile. He tapped his wand against my chin and I pushed him away, irritated by his over-familiarity.

"I was always taught to control my emotions at school. The teachers there told us it was a sure-fire way of sending your magick askew. We practised endlessly." I remembered the drills. Rather like learning our multiplication tables but with spells instead. We did all the basic skills repeatedly until we could do them in our sleep - do them without thinking.

Silvan chuckled. "But how old were you then? Seven, eight? No older, I'll warrant. The problem with school is that our young ones are sent there to be controlled. To be manipulated. You're coerced to behave in certain ways." He circled me, tapping his wand against my scalp. I flicked it away with my fingers. "They keep you in line. Insist on your obedi-ence. Teach you to tame the wildness within your soul. And they tell you that when you control your emotions, you perform clean magick."

He faced me, "And that's what you're doing,

Alfhild." He directed the tip of his wand at the banana I held in my hand. "You practise clean magick. It's neat. It's tidy. And it is largely ineffective." The banana slipped away from my hands and bobbed in the air in front of me. With another wiggle of Silvan's wand it spun in the air, dancing for my entertainment. "It's only when you properly let go, when you give free rein to your passion that magick becomes stronger."

That made sense. I thought of my friend Mara, a witch who lived deep in the forest with her faery changeling. Only last Christmas I'd witnessed the way that her emotions could cause adverse weather conditions. She could wreak storms over East Devon by virtue of feeling a tad fed-up. When she suffered a bereavement, we'd nearly had to cancel all the Inn's festivities. She'd wrought a snowmageddon that had brought the countryside to its knees.

"It goes against everything I've been taught to just let go and... throw magick around willy-nilly."

Silvan directed the banana back into my hands. "When I first met you in *The Web and Flame*, you were angry and desperate."

I nodded, mute. What could I say?

"Presumably you still are? You wouldn't have invited me here and offered to pay me a ridiculous sum of money if everything was alright in your world."

Thoughts of George were never far away, along with the horror of finding Derek Pearce dead in his cottage. And what of Mr Bramble, felled by a heart attack at the Psychic and Holistic Fayre held in Whittlecombe at Easter? And Rob Parker, sausage seller extraordinaire, who had lost his impressively-liveried van, but had fortunately been saved before he met a similar sizzling fate to his famous bangers.

George had been a hero that day. I would never give up looking for him.

Plus it wouldn't surprise me that there were countless other victims of The Mori.

So yes, it's fair to say I was angry.

Silvan tapped my chin with his wand again. My irritation flared and overflowed. I cast it out of his hand, with a spark of annoyance, and watched as it spun, end over end, hitting a beam and breaking neatly in two, both parts rolling into the narrow eaves of the attic. It would be a bit of stretch to reach in and pull them out, but of course Silvan didn't need to reach down. He simply beckoned and they came soaring through the air towards him.

"I'm so sorry." I watched him examine the broken ends.

"Don't be!" He waved them at me. "Nothing a little Sellotape won't fix. I'll send to Celestial Street for a replacement."

"I'll pay for it."

Silvan sniggered. "I'll add it to your bill." He wagged one half of the wand at me. "But do you see, Alfhild? How that little bit of negative energy gave your magick an edge? If you put a lid on your feelings and only perform clean magick, you will never know the real power of the forces you are engaging with."

He pointed at the banana in my hand. "Imagine that is The Mori. The man responsible for the disappearance of your detective friend." He moved to my side, standing just behind my shoulder. "Channel your feelings. Funnel them. Harness that energy inside you. Let it build." From behind me, I heard the sound of him taking a deep breath. "Oh that's good, I can feel it."

I did as he said, allowing the bleak feelings and despair I stored inside me to bubble and roil like hot sticky tar. I directed my frustration and grief at the banana, and as I did so, the yellow skin began to bruise and turn to brown, and then blacken. The banana aged in seconds, became droopy in my hand before collapsing on itself and falling to the floor with a dull splat.

"Nicely done," Silvan praised me. He moved to stand in front of me once more and tossed his own banana my way.

I caught it and examined its pristine flesh. "You're expecting me to do that to people though?"

Silvan raised an eyebrow. "Problem?"

"I'm not sure I have it in me."

"If you always do, what you've always done, you will always achieve the same results." He flicked the banana from my hand using a broken half of his wand. It hovered in the air between us. "Now, again. Try and take the banana away from me."

No more 'nice Alf'. Wasn't that what I'd said?

With a new sense of ferocity I beckoned the banana my way. It was almost in my hand before Silvan whipped it away.

"Excellent! We'll make a dark witch of you yet!"

CHAPTER FOUR

I 'd taken to spending a lot of my free time—and to be fair when you're running an inn, there isn't a great deal of that—walking around Whittlecombe and the surrounding area. My reason for doing this, ostensibly, was simply to make sure I was getting enough exercise. However, I think deep down, I continued to search for signs of George, or clues as to his whereabouts. I'd scrutinize every stranger I met, engage them in conversation, digging for information about who they were and their motives for visiting the little village.

I'd lived in Whittlecombe for a little over a year, and I'd noticed how I'd become increasingly alive to its innate energy. The more I trundled down the lanes or circumnavigated the village green and the large village pond, the more deeply acquainted I became with the profound magick at the centre of the village. I haunted Whittle Folly and the woods and marshes behind it, and grew increasingly familiar with the community and the rhythms of daily life.

The notion that something special and ancient existed within the land here had first occurred to me in the days after my dunking in the village pond at the hands of The Mori. The sprites or ghosts, or spirit water witches as I liked to think of them, had saved my life that awful night. It now seemed obvious to me that it was no coincidence that my wonky inn teemed with spirits. Whittlecombe was alive with its own magickal history and, like it or not, the villagers who made up the small community were part and parcel of that.

And so my forays into the lanes, mapping the village in its entirety, helped keep me fit on one level, but added fuel to the fire of my drive to understand this particular part of the British Isles and the lure it held for the Daemonne family. We'd lived here for hundreds and hundreds of years. Whittle Inn had been standing for five hundred years or so, and simply been added to in order to create its own inimitable wonky architecture.

After all those years in London, I really couldn't

imagine living anywhere else now. I felt at home here.

And I had no intention of being driven away from my ancestral home by a bunch of nasty wizards or warlocks.

Whittle Folly was as far as I could walk from the inn and still remain in Whittlecombe. The road here carried on and headed for Durscombe on the coast. I liked to walk down to the Folly and see how they were getting on with rebuilding the scout hut—a community funding initiative had provided the money needed to underpin the ground here and shore up the surrounding area. The council intended to replace the hut and make improvements to the parking area.

Behind the hut the forest spread out in all directions. It radiated out beyond a small housing development and the village, around the back of Whittle Lane, all the way up to Whittle Inn and beyond, with only the narrow road cutting through it. There were several springs running through the wood that originated in Speckled Wood, and they fed some of the marshy areas. The marshes were, for the most part, well signposted to ensure unsuspecting hikers didn't come to a dank, damp end by meandering into the water when they were unprepared to do so.

Everyone's favourite part of the Folly was the deep-water pool, however. During the summer, it provided a welcome respite on hot sunny days. Local kids loved diving into the clear water and cooling off. A local folk tale told that the pool was bottomless, but during the hot summer the previous year, the water had declined to a low level never previously seen—well not in living memory anyway—and it transpired it was fifteen feet deep at its centre.

My daily route habitually took me down as far as the Folly. On dry days I would circle the pool and then head back to the inn, with a stop at Whittle stores to say hello to Rhona and Stan. Then perhaps I'd call in briefly to see Millicent and her pooches, Sunny the Yorkshire Terrier and Jasper the lurcher.

Today should have been no different. Beautifully blues skies and warm air on a Saturday meant that the popular local beauty spot was relatively busy. As I walked across the car park, picking my way through the vehicles left there, I could hear a woman shrieking from the direction of the pool. I picked up my pace, alert to any other danger around me.

As I neared the pool itself, I could see where families had been sitting enjoying the day. Camping stools and collapsible chairs, picnic blankets, towels and hampers were spread around. People were clustering around the pool and I broke into a run and raced to join the small throng, willing to offer any assistance.

As I arrived at the pool's edge, I saw a child being pulled from the water and into his mother's outstretched arms. The look of relief on her face was palpable.

"What happened?" I asked the young man nearest me.

"The little lad got into trouble. He was playing on his own and maybe he slipped or something. I'm not sure."

"He lost his footing," his partner told me, her hand clamped over her heart. "He disappeared under the water and nobody noticed initially."

"Oh my goodness," I exclaimed.

The young woman whispered conspiratorially to me, "I think his mum was on her phone. She wasn't watching him."

"It's easily done." Her partner gave her a withering look.

"You need eyes in the back of your head, don't you?" I offered, trying to soothe relations between the two and the chap nodded sagely.

"Fortunately, Stan from the shop was here, and he leapt right in. Didn't think twice." The man indicated a fully-dressed Stan. He was wading out of the water to cheers and greetings from the gathered ensemble. We all broke into a round of spontaneous applause and Stan beamed and waved us away.

The mother of the half-drowned boy effusively offered her thanks and a few people patted him on the back. "It was nothing, really. Anyone would have done the same."

Pleased that everything had turned out for the best, I was about to continue on my way when I noticed that the normally clear water in the pool had assumed a strange reddy-coloured rusty hue. Half deciding it had been caused by Stan and the child disturbing the silt at the bottom of the pool, I wanted to dismiss what I was seeing, but something—some sixth sense—told me not to be too hasty. I slowly made my way to the edge of the pool and knelt beside it, dipping my fingers into the water.

The tingle I felt, like a small electric shock, could have been the skin and nerves of my hand reacting to the coolness of the water, of course it could, but remembering the time I'd felt the same odd sensation while out walking with Wizard Shadowmender, I had my doubts. I agitated the water once more, dragging my fingers through the silt, and observed the muddy brown colour the water turned. Not red. Not rust.

Decidedly odd.

"Well done, Stan," someone behind me was saying. "We need to get you home and into some dry clothes."

"Let him borrow a towel, somebody?" a woman suggested.

"Stan are you okay?" A third voice.

"I'm fine," Stan said. The wobble in his voice drew me upright—the water all but forgotten—just as he keeled over. I gasped in surprise and made a dash forward as his knees buckled beneath him, but others were there before me, catching him before he hit the ground.

"Oh, Stan," I gasped. Usually a healthy-looking man, his colouring had turned to grey, and even his lips were a little blue.

"Hypothermia?" A man asked uncertainly.

"Surely he wasn't in the water long enough?" I answered. "Call an ambulance. He doesn't look well at all."

"I will!" a woman shouted as everyone reached for their phones.

I grabbed Stan's hand. "You'll be fine, Stan," I told him. Maybe it was his heart.

"Rhona," he said, his voice weak, his eyes losing focus.

"I'll tell her," I said. "We'll call her now." Glancing behind me I asked, "Can someone call his wife. The number is 522 422. Her name is Rhona."

"The ambulance is coming," the first woman relayed to us.

"Oh no!" Another commotion off to the side of me. I heard a woman calling out, "Gregory? Gregory?"

Stan had drifted into unconsciousness and I leaned over to try and hear whether he was still breathing. As far as I could make out he was. I remembered George helping Mr Bramble in similar circumstances. He knew how to take a pulse and perform compressions. I could copy what he had done, if push came to shove, unless one of the other bystanders knew what they were doing.

"The little boy has collapsed too!"

Horrified, I tore my eyes from Stan only to see the child, Gregory, on the floor. His mother, her face as pale as her son's, eyes wide in shock, clutched at her child, while a bystander gently slapped the boy's cheeks.

What on earth were we dealing with here? Literally seconds ago both the boy and Stan had seemed fine.

I looked across at the shimmering pool next to me, the surface rippling inexplicably. "It's the water," I said. "There's something wrong with the water."

CHAPTER FIVE

"What do you mean there's something wrong with the water?" Gwyn quizzed me over dinner that evening. Not that she was eating you understand. Ghosts don't eat. But I was. Or at least I had been pushing my food around the plate while Monsieur Emietter looked on quizzically in the background. Used to seeing me with a healthy appetite, I'm not sure he really understood my sudden disinterest in food.

"The water quality around Whittlecombe has always been of an exceptionally high standard."

I regarded my great grandmother with some scepticism. I'm sure the water quality around Whittlecombe had always been wonderful, but you know how it is with some folk, they become very biased about the place they live and assume everywhere else is inferior. "I'm certain it still is, Grandmama. Well, for the most part. But quite clearly something made the little boy—Gregory he was called—very sick, And Stan too!"

"Then it will be localised to the pond at Whittle Folly." Gwyn sounded very sure of herself. "I really see no need for alarm."

I puffed my cheeks out. "I'm not so sure. I'm no scientist—"

"You might have been if you'd concentrated on your alchemy lessons in school—"

Alchemy? Grandmama could be so last century. "Grandmama!"

"Only an observation, my dear. Carry on with what you were saying."

I placed my fork down on the plate and lifted my hand to show her my fingers. "When Wizard Shadowmender was here I noticed something strange at the pool in Speckled Wood. The water seemed slightly... I don't know how to describe it... electrified."

"Electrified?" Gwyn looked puzzled.

"Grandmama, you know perfectly well what electricity is. Did you never have a little electric shock while you were alive?"

"I'm not sure I did, thank goodness. It sounds remarkably unpleasant."

I smiled. "A mild one is not very painful. But slightly disconcerting. The best way to describe it is as if someone was flicking you quite hard with their finger. It can have a real kick to it. There's some pain, although not a lot."

"And you felt that in the pool in Speckled Wood?"

I laid my knife down, deciding I'd finished eating. Monsieur Emietter frowned at me. "Something like that," I told Gwyn. "It was an odd sensation."

"Did you see anything?"

Something in Gwyn's voice made me pay attention to her properly. As I looked up at her she altered her features, presenting a face of complete neutrality.

"See anything? Like what?" I frowned at her, curious as to what she meant.

She simply shrugged. "I don't know. Anything that might cause that sort of feeling?"

That hadn't been what she'd been thinking, I was sure of it. "No. I thought maybe it was an eel, but there are no eels in that pond. Why would there be?" I considered what I had seen. "There was a little disturbance on the water. I thought it might have been a bird or an insect, but other than that, nothing."

"And yesterday? When you were at the Folly?"

"Similar sensation." I remembered the tinged water. "But the water had an odd hue. A rusty red colour, but you could only see it when you looked at it from a low angle."

"So there may well be something in the water that's caused Stan and the little boy to become ill?"

"Yes. Some sort of contamination," I agreed. "But that doesn't explain that sensation I experienced, does it?"

"No," Gwyn replied loftily and suddenly apparated away without so much as a by-your-leave, leaving me alone, with an almost-full plate of food in front of me, and a disgruntled Monsieur Emietter.

We eyed each other in confusion. "What was all that about?" I asked him but given his lack of command of the English language, he was no help whatsoever.

"Inspector Norbert Kerslake, Madam. Pleased to make your acquaintance." The small man standing stock still in front of the bar nodded at me and cast a sidelong glance at Florence who had shown him in, taking in her smouldering clothes and noticeable translucence. He looked back at me, probably hoping for a behavioural cue, unsure as to what he was seeing.

"Alfhild Daemonne," I introduced myself and hurried to the other side of the bar to shake his hand. "Welcome to Whittle Inn, Inspector Kerslake." In turn, I looked him up and down. A dark grey suit, smart white shirt, subdued tie. A pair of round glasses perched on the end of his nose. A pen in his jacket pocket, sturdy boots and a yellow hard hat tucked under his arm. A briefcase in his other hand. Not a policeman. So what then? "How can I help you?"

"I'm from the Devon and Cornwall Water Board, Madam. We're currently collecting water samples from all around the Whittlecombe area. Whittle Inn falls into our geographical target area and I'll therefore need access to any and all water outlets."

"Oooh!" Florence put her hand to her mouth in concern, wafting the smell of scorched cotton towards Norbert. He crinkled his nose. "Is the water alright? Only we have guests staying here at the moment."

"What happened to you, Miss?" Norbert asked. "Should you be working?"

Florence blinked. "What on earth do you mean?" she asked in confusion. "It's not my day off."

"Florence, Florence, I'll handle this," I interjected, and nodded my head in the direction of the kitchen.

My housekeeper sniffed but accepted the hint. Unfortunately she also took umbrage, as well as a short cut to the kitchen, by walking through the walls to get there.

Norbert did a double take and followed that with a few steps backwards. "How the—"

"Ah yes. Erm—" I pondered on what to say. "We're a themed inn, Inspector Kerslake. We have a number of, erm, parlour tricks, and optical illusions, just to keep the guests on their toes. You know? Ha ha ha." I smiled as though there was nothing strange going on. "I hope you won't find us too weird. And er... just ignore anything untoward."

He blinked at me owlishly, through the thick lenses of his spectacles. "I see." Clearly he didn't.

"With this being an inn, we have quite a few bathrooms. Do you need to visit each of them?" I asked, hurriedly moving on to the matter in hand.

"That's why I decided it would be pertinent if I

attended this property myself. Half of my team are visiting all the domestic residences in the town; the other half are looking in the woods and forests in the vicinity. I elected to attend to The Hay Loft and Whittle Inn myself."

"If you want a job doing well, eh?"

"Precisely." Norbert didn't crack a smile. "Yes, I'll need to see every tap in the house, plus the water tank if you have one in the attic. I'll need to assess every water inlet and outlet, dishwasher, washing machine... those sorts of things. I'll require all the covers taken off the drains and then I'll need to look at any outside taps you may have. I believe your grounds are fairly extensive?"

The man was a jobsworth for sure. "Yes. In addition to the gardens, the woods at the rear of the property belong to the estate."

"Any pools, marshy areas out there?"

"Oh yes indeed, plenty." After the heavy snow we'd had at Christmas and the torrential rain after Easter, this peculiar little man had his work cut out.

Nothing is ever as simple as you imagine it's going to be, is it?

Norbert changed into a lab jacket and a pair of goggles and spent the next few hours gathering samples from every tap he could find. I watched him from a distance as he methodically labelled every single test tube by hand and filed them in a portable rack he kept in a large leather-bound wheelie case.

Certainly, Inspector Kerslake had enough on his plate indoors, but what we hadn't banked on was the fact that once upon a time there had been a pair of wells. The first of these we knew about, situated as it was at the rear of the inn, near where the outbuildings were. It had long been filled in and covered over, but a cursory examination of the site located it.

What was more alarming was that the inn itself appeared to have been built over the second well, or at least it had housed the well in what was now the beer cellar. Despite my protestations, Inspector Kerslake insisted on bringing in another of his infernal teams to excavate both of these wells in order to take samples. Excavation in this case, it turned out, meant installing a huge drill in the cellar and going down through the floor.

"What is the point?" I'd asked in dismay. "If the wells are covered up, no-one will be drinking out of them."

"That's a rather simplistic view to take, Miss

Daemonne," Norbert replied. "They may filter into the water table and infect other supplies. We need to be thorough in our investigations."

I nodded, more than a little grumpy, knowing that the consequent disruption would be sure to drive me and many of the inhabitants of the inn to the brink of insanity. For her part, Charity had taken to performing her duties while wearing noise cancelling headphones. Many of the ghosts had disappeared altogether. I hadn't seen Gwyn since our conversation over dinner, so I assumed she had escaped somewhere quiet, although I had a sneaking suspicion that she was avoiding me.

"You know that little man is seriously getting on my nerves right now," Silvan said to me. A late riser, Silvan tended to stay up until well into the early hours and then rise at midday. It had taken some getting used to on my part, because I was up with the lark—or the owl—every morning before the dawn. I had to ensure our guests had the breakfast they desired and make sure the inn was ready for another day of hospitality. I'd been hoping to receive instruction from Silvan as soon as the breakfast service had been finished, but instead I had to wait until after lunch, for it was only then, after copious amounts of coffee, that he felt ready to face the world.

Today I'd stumbled on him when I walked past his room just after 9.30 am. I was heading to my office to catch up on some paperwork, but the water workmen had arrived and now the walls of the inn vibrated along to the deep bass thrumming sound of the drills in the cellar. The noise made two fillings in my back teeth rattle.

As I'd walked along the passage that ran between the guest bedrooms on the second floor I'd had to steady myself with my hands against the walls.

Silvan appeared in the hallway wearing black pyjamas and a pink silk eye mask. He'd tied his hair up on his head and looked markedly different from his usual self. I couldn't help but stare.

A burst of drilling had us both cringing, the whine reverberating loudly throughout the inn. "I am sorry for the disruption," I told him, when I could finally make myself heard. I truly was. Silvan was not paying to stay at the inn, but he was still my guest. "I'm hoping they'll finish off what they need to do today and then we'll all get some peace." If it went on much longer some of my guests would be inclined to leave early, that much was certain.

Another burst of drilling. I winced and began to walk past him, but he reached a hand out and stopped me. "What is the issue here?" he asked.

"A contaminated water supply. Well, I say that, but I don't know for certain. That's what they suspect. They haven't released anything official yet."

"The water at the inn?"

"No, in Whittlecombe generally."

"In the pipes?"

I shrugged. "I really don't know. There's a large natural pool of water out near Whittle Folly. A couple of people who were in the water a few days ago have been taken ill. The inspectors from the water board have found something they don't like and so they're checking the whole water supply around the village. And standing water too."

We waited for another excruciating staccato burst of whining and throbbing to pass. "Oh." Silvan rubbed his face and yawned. "So how long will they be drilling for? My head is vibrating."

"It can't be much longer." I sought to reassure him as much as myself. "They must be through to the centre of the earth by now."

"I'd be careful what you wish for. Maybe we'll all be caught up in a gush from a geyser of molten lava."

As the drilling started up again, and the paintings on the walls in the passageway jigged up and down, I rubbed my temples and thought that might not be such a bad end.

Silvan stretched. "Anyhow, seeing as I'm awake, let's get to work shall we? I'll meet you in the attic in twenty minutes. Bring coffee."

I nodded my assent and tried to remember what I'd been doing before I was waylaid.

"And painkillers," Silvan called after me as I walked away and the drill started up once more. "Bring plenty of those."

"Again! Again!"

From behind me, Silvan threw half a dozen coloured silk handkerchiefs up in the air. As I whirled around they danced, weaving rapidly in and out of each other. My task was simply to isolate the red one and set it on fire. I missed and succeeded only in singeing the wall.

"Urgh!" I bent over, hands on my knees, catching my breath, my forehead clammy, my hair everywhere. Silvan practised a very physical form of magick, that seemed to involve a fair number of fencing moves. Most of the magick I'd learned as a youngster had involved standing still and directing energy at an object. Now here I was, expected to prance around like a Viennese horse.

"Come, come, Alfhild. Don't fall asleep on the job." Silvan tapped me with his wand. He'd wrapped Sellotape around the break, which seemed a little incongruous, but it still appeared to be working alright.

"I can't do it," I moaned. "I'm finding it hard to hit the target when it and I are both moving. One of us needs to be still."

Silvan gave me such a look of pitiful disparagement that my toes almost curled up in response. "Because your enemies will remain still, will they?" he sneered.

"No—" I thought of the spinning globes of The Mori, darting here and there in Speckled Wood on the night we had battled them.

"And you? Will you be remaining in one place?"

"I—"

"You'll either be running towards them or running away from them. Either way they will want to kill you, so you will need to return the favour." Silvan folded his arms. "That's about the shape of it."

I stood straight and stretched. "You're right." I hated to admit that he was, but you couldn't fault his logic.

"You know, you could consider finding yourself a wand," Silvan suggested.

I curled my lip. "I've never found one I liked. Nothing that worked for me."

"Well keep looking, my love." I bristled at Silvan's familiarity. "I think it would improve your directionality no end. You have hands as clumsy as bear paws."

"Thank you," I said, thoroughly insulted.

"You're welcome."

I lifted my hands up into the attack stance Silvan had been drumming into me. The man irritated me beyond reason.

"Again!" I ordered, pointing at the silk handker-chiefs. "Again!"

Later we lay on the floor of the attic. My shoulders and thighs burned with the unaccustomed stretch-ing, the pushing and pulling of energy around the room. Even my fingers felt stiff. I lifted my hands and examined them, palms facing and then away. The ring George had given me for my birthday glittered in the light spilling in on us from the large round window that faced out onto the gardens.

Silvan caught my hand and studied the ring too.

"That's an interesting choice of adornment." The scathing tone in his voice was unmistakeable.

"It's an engagement ring. George was proposing before he disappeared."

Silvan grunted with amusement. "Marriage." He obviously didn't approve. "It's all about ownership."

I pulled my hand away.

"May I see it?" he asked.

"No," I said, feeling suddenly self-conscious.

"Take it off. Let me have a look."

"No!" I rolled away from him and stood up. "You're just jealous."

Silvan laughed. "Jealous? Of what? That you have an expensive piece of bling on your finger, or that you're owned by someone else?"

I growled at him. "I am *not* owned by George or anyone else."

Silvan pushed himself up on one elbow. "But when you give yourself away to another you are no longer free."

"I disagree. When you're in love it's the greatest feeling in the world. You can do anything. You have someone watching your back, someone encouraging you, someone supporting you. Someone there for you when it all goes wrong. You feel invincible. Isn't that something wonderful?"

Silvan narrowed his eyes. "I'm already invincible."

Such confidence the man had. I admired him for that.

"You've never loved?" I asked him.

He sat up, his elbows on his knees, his hair flopping over his eyes. "Of course I have, Alfhild. And deeply. Believe it or not." Something flickered in his eyes. I wanted to know more but didn't feel I could pry.

"There you are then." I sounded like a petulant child.

"Love makes you weak, Alfhild. It's the thin end of a wedge that can be used to crack open the door before bludgeoning you to death."

"Now there's a cheery thought," I scolded, annoyed at his dismissal of my emotions.

"I'm serious. Deadly serious." He tapped the side of his head. "The Mori know you too well. They know how you react. They can force you into a situation and they will expect you to behave in predictable ways."

That thought drew me up short.

"Why do they know you so well?" Silvan asked.

"Jed." I spat the word out with complete contempt. "When I first moved into the inn I enlisted the help of a local painter, decorator, odd-job man. He—" I took a deep breath, ashamed of how I'd been hoodwinked. "He rapidly became important to me. I thought it was..." I trailed off.

"Love," Silvan finished for me, the word stark, hanging in the air between us. The insinuation being that I was a weak-minded fool.

I nodded and remained quiet.

"You thought you loved this Jed?" Silvan's voice was not without sympathy.

"Yes. But he was a member of The Mori. He pulled the wool over my eyes."

"And then this George came along and now you think you love him too?"

"I know I do," I snapped.

"In the space of twelve months, you've loved two men." It was a wry observation, not meant cruelly, but it struck home. *Was it so wrong to fall for them both?* My eyes filled with tears.

Silvan casually tossed the red silk handkerchief into the air. It darted away from us, skipping between the low beams above our heads. "Those rocks on your finger weigh your magick down, Alfhild," he said, his voice gentle.

The handkerchief rushed out into the open and I directed a beam of pure hatred its way. It burst into flames, burning for a fraction of a second with a phosphorescent sparkle until all that remained were minute ash particles floating in the air.

"Bravo," Silvan said, in much the same soft tone he had used before. "Now again."

CHAPTER SIX

T he village hall, packed to the rafters, was standing room only. Fortunately Millicent had arrived ahead of me, without her dogs for once, and had bagged me a seat on the far right-hand side. I squeezed past people, waving and smiling at those I knew, and trying not to stand on anybody's toes.

"How's your drilling going?" Millicent asked, as I slid into the seat next to her with a sigh of relief. All the bodies in the hall were making it very warm. I fanned myself, looking longingly at the glazed windows, set well above head height in the walls, hoping someone would open them. As usual I had been running late, so had rushed into the village and was hot and flustered as a result.

I shook my head, a pained look on my face. "Can you believe they're still doing it? Well not now, obviously. They clock off at five. But they'll be back tomorrow at half eight. Honestly Millicent! Are they hoping to discover oil? What can they be doing down there?"

"Have you been into the cellar and investigated?"

About to blithely say 'no, why would I have? It's only the water board after all', I bit back the words. No I hadn't been down and had a look. I met Millicent's eyes and she pulled a face. "Surely they wouldn't be doing anything untoward down there?" I asked instead.

Millicent nodded knowingly. "Always best to check these things out."

"You're right," I said. "But under our noses...?" I couldn't see it myself.

"Order, order." The imperious figure of my old adversary Gladstone Talbot-Lloyd appeared on the raised stage at the front of the hall, and the hubbub in the room decreased noticeably.

"What's he doing here?" I hissed.

Millicent giggled and leaned close to me to whisper, "I hear he's intending to stand as the local parliamentary candidate for East Devon."

"No!" I was scandalised.

"He has all the right connections and qualifications for the job."

"But he has no interest in the locals of Whittle-combe, let alone anyone else. Talbot-Lloyd is all about himself and the money he can make from dodgy deals."

Millicent laughed again, a little too loudly. "He's the perfect candidate for Westminster then, isn't he?"

"Sssssssssssssh!" A woman in the row in front of us hissed, and suitably chastised, Millicent and I sat back in our seats and began to pay attention to the meeting as it got underway.

Talbot-Lloyd was in full flow thanking the village hall committee for the loan of the hall, and to the WI for giving up the space on what would normally have been their evening. "Most of all I'd like to thank Chief Inspector Kerslake from the Devon and Cornwall Water Board for coming here this evening to give us a rundown of what's happening." A ripple of applause and Norbert came to the front of the stage to shake Talbot-Lloyd's hand.

Hmpf, I thought.

Norbert smiled at Talbot-Lloyd, "My absolute pleasure."

"Without further ado, ladies and gentlemen, Chief Inspector Kerslake."

Another smattering of applause. Beads of sweat

were breaking out on my forehead. I dabbed at my face with a tissue. Behind us, somebody had closed the front doors. I was going to bake or suffocate in very short order.

Norbert cleared his throat. "As you will all be aware, I've had several teams performing a great many tests on the water in and around Whittle-combe village and surrounds. I have some prelimi-nary findings that I would very much like to share with you. Once I've done that, I will explain what we will be doing to improve matters, before opening the floor up for questions and discussion."

A general buzz of anticipation spread throughout the hall, and Norbert looked around at the people seated in front of him with interest. We gazed back at him in anticipation.

I waved at my face, ineffectually with my tissue. The room was completely airless. *Get on with it!* I screamed inwardly. Millicent shot a glance at me. I rolled my eyes.

Norbert consulted his notes. "As suspected there has been a high level of contaminant found in the pool near Whittle Folly, and exposure to this conta-minant was undoubtedly the reason that two members of the community were taken so poorly last week. This is entirely regrettable, and we wish to pass on our best wishes to the families involved, and of course we hope that both parties make a full recovery." There were general murmurs of agreement.

"Hear hear!" A call from the far left of the room.

I looked over that way out of idle interest and did a double take.

Surely it couldn't be. Was that ...? Yes.

Gwyn was standing on the far side, among the crowd who didn't have seats. Could I be imagining things? I had never known Gwyn venture out of the inn, although she did have a tendency to disappear for long periods of time and I could never be sure where she had gone.

But here she was, dressed in her blue velvet finery, a little translucent, and solemn-faced.

What had brought her here?

Norbert began speaking again. "Now we had anticipated that whatever caused the contamination in the pool at the Folly location would be contained." Norbert glanced down at his notes once more, and then back up. The audience stared back at him, eager for more details. You didn't have to be a psychic to anticipate what he was going to say next.

"Unfortunately, this hasn't been the case."

As one, people began turning to their neighbours exclaiming at the news.

"We've found traces of the same contaminant in all the standing water around Whittlecombe."

"Everywhere?" Someone in the audience called.

Norbert nodded, looking gravely down at the man who had interrupted. "So far, yes. Every marsh area in the woods, every pool and pond—including the village pond—and in every well."

I sat up straight. *In every well? Including the wells at Whittle Inn?*

"What about the water supply to our houses?" A woman asked, a note of hysteria creeping in.

Norbert held his hands up. "One thing at a time, please."

"I have kids!" The woman retorted angrily, and a brief look of irritation passed across Norbert's face.

"I appreciate that, Madam," he retorted.

"Answer the question," another woman called out. The threat of pandemonium hung in the air. I glanced around. You couldn't blame people for worrying, especially those mothers with young cubs to look after. I could see a few of those in the crowd.

"Order!" Talbot-Lloyd called officiously, no doubt enjoying his role in the meeting immensely. He was the man wielding all the power.

"Very well," Norbert held his hands up in a placating gesture. "At this time, we believe that the water supplied directly from the Water Board is not a cause for concern." This statement was met with a wave of relief. "However, we intend to take precautions," Norbert continued, and the audience grew still again. "We'll be bringing in our own standpipe system and tankers full of water. We would encourage you to make use of our provision rather than use your own water until further notice. The resources will be refreshed daily for the foreseeable future."

People began talking among themselves again. There was an air of excitement in the air, probably because this was something new for the village.

"I'll take questions now." Norbert smiled serenely.

Talbot-Lloyd quickly joined the inspector at the front of the stage and clapped his hands to garner everyone's attention. "Shall we go through the chair?" he asked. "Yes, you Sir, in the checked shirt. What's your question?"

"Can you say what the contamination actually is?" Rob Parker, sausage seller extraordinaire asked.

"And how dangerous is it?" yelled a female voice from somewhere behind me.

"Order!" Talbot-Lloyd interjected forcefully.

Norbert consulted his notes. "To answer both of

these questions... let me see. Yes." He looked up. "All I can tell you at this stage is that it is a chemical contaminant. Something rather nasty. We haven't been able to isolate the exact components of that, but we will be making that a top priority in our labs over the next few days and coming weeks, if need be." That didn't sound good. Chemicals in the water. I guessed it could have come from some pesticide spill on a farm, maybe.

"As for how dangerous it is, well, you probably all know that two members of the community are being cared for in intensive care at the Royal Devon and Exeter Hospital, so we are aware that this is a very serious threat to public health and that's why we're taking it seriously."

"What happens if it spreads further?" An older man asked.

"How much further could it spread?" his neighbour argued. "It's already in all the marshes and ponds. That's what the man said."

The older man flushed. "I mean, could it get into the pipes?"

Norbert nodded round at everyone, his face extremely serious "That's always a possibility. Once these things leech into the water table they can be difficult to get to grips with, but obviously we are doing everything in our power to contain this spillage."

"How on earth has this come about?" A vocal man in the front row asked.

"Where did it start?"

"Who's responsible?"

A chorus of voices demanded answers that Norbert could not possibly have the answers to, and yet he chose that moment to look directly at me, and all of a sudden my stomach flipped over. Up until then, I hadn't been aware he had even noticed I was here, but that glance was meaningful. He had singled me out.

"We believe the source is from a spring that starts at the north end of Speckled Wood, on land belonging to Whittle Inn."

For a second you could have heard a pin drop in the hall. Then people were shouting, and chairs were being scraped back. Angry faces looked my way, fingers were pointed accusingly. I sat where I was, mute with shock.

"That's absurd!" Millicent was on her feet. "You can't possibly know that's the case."

People shouted over her, drowning out her protestations. On the stage Talbot-Lloyd had stepped back into the shadows. He wasn't calling the meeting to order now. Far from it. He was allowing the mob to be fuelled by fire. Norbert had lit the touch paper and now he and Talbot-Lloyd would stand well back while my reputation burned.

Here, if the village needed it, was yet one more reason for them to hate Whittle Inn and its inhabitants. The clarity of my next thought startled me.

"It's a lie," I said, not loud enough for anyone else to hear. "I've been set up."

I remembered the empty bags I'd seen when I was being held at Piddlecombe Farm. George had told me they contained chemicals. The same chemicals that had previously been stored in the shed at Derek Pearce's allotment. There was no doubt in my mind that those chemicals had been used by The Mori to contaminate the water around Whittle Inn.

Somebody behind me jostled my shoulder, not in a nice way. Someone else caught at my hair. Schoolground bullying. Pathetic and I didn't need to rise to it, but the embers of my hatred for The Mori had been properly stoked.

I stood, drawing myself up, casting a sideways glance at Gwyn. She looked back at me, her face equally grim. I could tell she knew I wanted to lash out. She shook her head, a minute movement that stalled any intention I might have had to create a scene.

She drew a wand out of a small velvet pouch she was carrying in lieu of a handbag. I'd never seen her with a wand before. In fact I'd never seen Gwyn perform magick. Until that moment I hadn't been aware that it was possible for ghosts to do so. She pointed it towards the top of the walls nearest her and flicked the tip. Every window suddenly burst outward, glass shattering, wood splintering, latches and metal stays ricocheting back and forth.

There was pandemonium. People shrieked and screamed, ducked, or threw themselves to the floor. As a flood of fresh air flooded the hall and provided much needed relief, some of the gathered crowd fled through the front doors and out into the street beyond.

Gwyn nodded at me... and disappeared.

On the stage, Talbot-Lloyd was trying to call the room to order, but that particular horse had bolted. I stared at him, with steely concentration, until he met my gaze. "Game on," I mouthed at him and he curled his lip into a sneer.

Millicent pulled at my arm. "Let's get out of here," she said and reluctantly I followed her, pushing my way through the crowds of people.

Passing through the front door, I found myself pelted with small stones. One hit me squarely on the forehead, and I ducked in surprise. I put my fingers up to where it was smarting and found blood. Turning angrily, I came face to face with Grace Gretchen.

"Witch," she hissed.

Is this what we'd come to? It was like the seventeenth century all over again.

CHAPTER SEVEN

M illicent, Charity, and I huddled at the kitchen table, whilst Gwyn—I'd like to say paced, but given her status as a ghost—*floated* backwards and forwards around the kitchen in an unusual display of agitation. Millicent for her part was furious. And while I found myself disturbed by the events that had unfolded in the village, I needed some time to ruminate on them too, so I held my tongue and simply thought about it all.

"It's quite obvious what they're trying to do," Charity was saying. "We have to set the record straight somehow, Alf."

"They're out-manoeuvring us at every turn," Gwyn said.

Charity ran her hands through her hair, currently coloured bright orange. "Do you think

Chief Inspector Kerslake was in on this the entire time?"

I frowned at the sound of the odious little man's name. "Almost definitely," I answered through gritted teeth. I'd been a fool not to see through him.

The back door rattled and we all jumped. Finbarr and Silvan entered—they'd been out, patrolling the boundary of Speckled Wood.

"Evening all." Finbarr's sing-song Irish accent interrupted our sudden silence. He glanced at each of us in turn. "Not a grand one by the look of it."

Silvan reached for a glass on the draining board and ran the water from the tap. "What's going on?"

"We've been set up by The Mori," I answered quickly, watching him as he took a drink. "They've poisoned the water around the village."

He spat the water into the sink. "All of the water?"

"Not the stuff in the taps apparently." I stood and took his glass from him, holding it to the light. Nothing to see. I handed the glass back to him and he poured it away. "They're claiming that the contamination started here at Whittle Inn and ran downstream, infiltrating the other water sources."

"Is that likely?" Silvan asked.

I shrugged, no expert on water after all. "We're

slightly higher up than the rest of the village here, so if the contamination originated here, it's feasible the run off would have affected lower lying areas I suppose."

"But to get from Speckled Wood to Whittle Folly?" Gwyn shook her head. She wasn't buying it.

"That's a good couple of miles, that, isn't it, now?" Finbarr said. He and I had walked the route together several times.

"And in any case not all of the water they're talking about is fed from the springs on this land. There's a lot of standing water that just gathers when it rains. Plenty of marshland in the woods," Millicent chipped in.

I folded my arms and leaned back against the worktop. "I think you're right. There can't surely be one single source for this contamination." I looked around at my friends. "You remember when I was abducted that last night at the Fayre? I came across some large plastic sacks in the outbuilding I was held in." Millicent, Gwyn and Charity obviously remembered the occasion clearly and Finbarr had heard me talk about it, but Silvan never had. He looked shocked as I continued. "I can't know for sure where it was, but George followed up on the assumption it was Piddlecombe Farm. He found the empty bags I'd seen—and in the daylight was able to say they had contained chemicals. Similar chemicals to those we found in Derek Pearce's shed. That was the last thing George was able to tell me before he had to hang up."

I breathed hard, feeling the weight of the grief permanently lodged in my heart. The others stared back at me with sympathy, their faces grave, reflecting my own feelings of anguish. "I'm willing to bet good money that those chemicals were used to contaminate the water. Do any of you think that's too far-fetched?"

Finbarr nodded his head slowly. "That's a good theory, like. But Alf, we've had Speckled Wood under protection this whole time, have we not? The Mori shouldn't have been able to access it and contaminate the water here."

He was right. I hadn't thought of that. I slumped. Maybe my theory was wrong then.

"You're missing a couple of fairly obvious red flags here," Silvan said, his eyes shadowed. "If Kerslake is involved, that means we don't have any independent proof that all of the water is contaminated. Not here on the estate or in fact anywhere else in Whittlecombe with the exception of Whittle Folly."

I nodded. "And?"

"If, as Kerslake told you, the water in the grounds and the woods around the inn has been contaminated, and you are assuming someone interfered with it purposely, then someone you trust will have been to blame. That's if all the work that Finbarr and your friends have done really does ensure the grounds of the inn cannot be breached." He nodded at Finbarr. "No offence, mate."

"None taken." Finbarr dipped his head at me. "Silvan makes a good point there, Alf."

I met Silvan's eyes. Bless his dark heart. Presumably it helped understand the deviousness in others if you were a scoundrel yourself.

"I can't believe one of us would have done that," Charity said in shock, and I had to agree with her. Silvan had me reconsidering everything I knew about my friends, and about everyone who had ever walked through the door of the inn.

Another traitor? Another betrayal?

Jed all over again.

The thought made my head ache.

Abruptly I swung away from them all and let myself out of the back door.

"Alf—" Millicent called after me, but I closed the

door forcefully, shutting them out of my life for a while.

I wanted to be alone.

With June just a few days away, there was plenty of warmth in the air, and still some light in the sky. The weather had been balmy after a wet spring, and so it seemed to me as I made my way up the back gardens of my wonky inn, heading as always for Speckled Wood, that the green of the grass and the hedges, and the canopy above the trees, was deeper and more magickal than ever. The raised flower beds that Ned and Zephaniah had planted out here looked spectacular in the glow of the setting sun, and the lazy buzzing of plump bumble bees—a sound of summer that brought me joy—was music to my ears.

But once I'd entered the dappled shade of the woods, I sensed a change. There was something I couldn't quite put my finger on. Not a sense of menace particularly, more an absence of light. It became so noticeable, that a few hundred yards into the wood I paused and engaged my senses properly.

I closed my eyes, standing straight and imagined my own feet rooting in the soil. I held my hands up in front of me, slightly out to the side, feeling them growing out through my spine, like a sunflower as it worships the sun. Straight away I scented a tang in the air, something vaguely metallic and out of place in this most natural of cathedrals. The more I became mindful of it the more noticeable it was. I could almost taste the unpleasantness on my tongue.

The second thing was a stillness that should not have been so apparent. Normally I could walk alone in Speckled Wood and without even consciously acknowledging the sound, I would hear small animals, insects and birds going about their business. That should have been especially so at this time of day, but although I strained to listen, the sounds of contented animals foraging, playing or settling down for the evening were absent.

Something was badly amiss.

Opening my eyes, I took a few tentative steps to a tree on my right. A Silver Birch. I lay my hand flat against its surface where the bark was peeling, feeling its coarseness under the palm of my hand, and I listened to the sound of life within. The heartbeat of the forest. It seemed strong enough. I thought...

So why was I worried?

I glanced around, my eye falling on a massive oak

tree close by covered in moss. I repeated the process I'd gone through with the Silver Birch, laying my hand flat, softly against the spongey moss, conscious of the delicate life below. This tree was ancient, with a girth of over twelve feet. I could hear it soaking up water from the ground, lapping like a thirsty dog.

Again, something didn't feel quite right.

My heart beat harder in my chest.

I turned to the north, knowing that night would soon be falling. Nonetheless I was a woman with a mission. A witch with a bad feeling. I followed the wider paths through the wood as quickly as I could, breaking into a jog from time to time. To my left I passed the large pool of water where I'd walked with Wizard Shadowmender and first felt the little bolt of electricity. Beyond that, there was more marshland between the trees. Some of those were areas with little more than dank puddles of rainwater, while others contained deep pools of water, the algae floating on the top, the water otherwise clear.

I bypassed them all, growing breathless as I raced for my destination, intent on arriving before dark, racing up the inclines. All the work I'd undertaken with Silvan meant I was fitter than I'd ever been, and that pleased me, but I recognised I had some way to go to be the wily wiry witch he desired me to be.

And finally I found what I was looking for. On the top of a fair-sized hill, a spring rose out of a mound in the ground, a large mossy hillock, surrounded by gnarled oaks and ash trees, and a smattering of pines, holly twisting on the trunks hereabouts.

I knelt alongside it on the soft ground, water bubbling and gurgling from a hole in the rocks. Tentatively I reached out and touched the water, part of me perhaps expecting my fingers to be burned in some sort of acid attack. The water was icy cold, but it was still just plain old H2o, devoid of fluoride or other additives, and my skin didn't react to it in any way.

I rocked back on my heels, peering about me. The light was failing now, the shadows growing longer. I observed the water as it trickled away, running over rocks and pebbles, merrily making its way south, heading for the marshes, disappearing from my sight as it bubbled over a mound of rocks where the ground fell away more steeply.

I cautiously clambered down the hill to the next levelling. Something caught my eye immediately. Plastic bags had been stuffed among the under-growth close to where the water tumbled off another ledge and pooled below. From the pool, the water spilled out, branching out in rivulets heading towards the marshland. I reached into the prickly branches and pulled out not one, but two large cream coloured heavy duty plastic sacks. Risking being scratched to death I poked around some more and found another couple.

I placed them on the ground and smoothed one of them out so that I could read the wording printed on the bag.

Halite.
High quality granular marine salt
25kg

Salt? 25kg seemed to be a lot of salt.

I opened one of the bags, and instantly reeled away from the acidic smell. Whatever had been in these bags it had not been common or garden rock salt.

I flipped the bag over to read the small lettering on the back.

Fast acting rock salt.
Conforms to BS 3247 1991
Easily spreadable
Perfect for car parks, drives and footpaths.

So absolutely no need for it in the woods. I wouldn't have used it here, even at the height of snowmageddon five months earlier.

Repeat use as necessary
Astutus Holdings
Whittlecombe, Devon

Astutus!

Proof if any were needed that The Mori were behind this. It made perfect sense to me that an organisation intent on destruction of the environment wouldn't blink at leaving their plastic rubbish behind, stuffed in the undergrowth. But this was clumsy. Stupid even.

They had to know it would be found. That I would find it. Or were they so arrogant that they didn't care at all?

I bundled the bags together, then carefully climbed down to the pool below. The water was murky, churned up, overflowing from the pool and rushing headlong into the woods below me, feeding the rest of the trees and all life that existed beyond this point.

I headed for home, this time more slowly, walking into the marshes. I could hear the buzz and hum of insects, the chirrup of crickets, and the croaking of frogs and toads – but much less than I might have expected. Every one of my senses was strung out, trying to process the overload of sensory information my witchy mind was receiving.

My heart was in my mouth. I knew that whatever had been in these bags had not been salt, and I understood that the water had been poisoned on purpose. Unless I did something quickly, Speckled Wood would succumb to the toxicity of whatever poison had been added to the water, along with every living creature—animal, insect and plant—for miles around.

CHAPTER EIGHT

B y the time I returned to the inn the kitchen was empty. I could hear chatter from the bar area and assumed that Charity was attending to our guests in there. Wanting to avoid everyone for now, I slipped up the backstairs without making my presence known and entered my rooms.

I kept my orb, wrapped in a velvet cloth for safekeeping, in a box tucked away in my wardrobe. I extracted it and carried the box to my window seat, perching there while I gently unwrapped the orb to set it on a cushion next to me. It caught the light from the rising moon, unleashing several bubbles, which sparkled and popped before the orb became still and waited.

I waved my right hand over the top. Clouds erupted from the base, billowing white and then dissipating like smoke that has been wafted gently aside.

Wizard Shadowmender's face appeared before me. He blinked at me and smiled, but I could see an underlying seriousness in his face.

"You have news, Alf?"

How much did he know? "I do."

"Millicent has been in touch this evening to discuss what happened at the meeting in Whittlecombe."

"It's The Mori."

"That's what she said."

I held up one of the plastic bags I'd brought home from the woods, so that he could see it. "I've been out in Speckled Wood this evening and I've found five of these empty plastic bags. Each of them holds 25kg of rock salt, but judging by the smell, whatever was in these bags was not salt. It can't have been."

Wizard Shadowmender scratched his beard, frowning in concentration. "This gets worse and worse."

"Someone has poisoned the spring that rises here in Speckled Wood. It's just one of several sources of water for my land. I'm willing to bet that each of them has received the same treatment." I exhaled, anxiety gnawing at my insides. "I checked at the source and the water that is flowing up to the ground seems pure. It's been contaminated at the point it exits the earth." I set the plastic bag down carefully. "The thing is, even if all the springs on my land have been polluted, it seems unlikely to me that my water will flow from the Whittle Estate and pollute Whittle Folly. It must have come from the forest beyond."

Wizard Shadowmender stared through the glass, his lips pinched grimly together.

"That means we have a wide-scale problem," I continued.

"We need to clean it up."

"We do. And quickly." I hesitated to tell him the worst of it. "I walked through Speckled Wood this evening and I took in the marshland. I'm fairly certain everything has been contaminated. I'll go back out at first light and look again. But I'm no ecologist, Wizard Shadowmender. And I'm no arboriculturalist, horticulturalist or biologist either. I need specialists here."

"I hear you, Alf," the elderly wizard nodded. "I'll see what I can do, but everyone I can think of is elsewhere at the moment, tied up with several other crises. I think for starters, you should make use of the people around you." I guessed he meant Millicent and Finbarr, but Millicent was a potionist and Finbarr a specialist in magickal defence. I couldn't see how much use either of them would be for me.

"Then there's the small matter that everyone in the village is going to hate me."

"Only if they believe the lies that are spread about you, and certainly not everyone will."

That was easy for Shadowmender to say, he hadn't been at the meeting. For now, I didn't want to contradict him, so I nodded.

"Get some sleep, Alf. Perhaps things won't look so bleak in the morning."

I forced a smile and waved my fingers as the clouds rolled across the orb.

I had a feeling that for once Wizard Shadow-mender was wrong. Things would be worse in the morning.

I tossed and turned all night, occasionally falling deeply asleep only to be catapulted from the land of nod by horrific dreams of mutant insects and dying trees. It seemed my subconscious was anticipating an apocalyptic end for the dozy village of Whittlecombe. I fell deeply asleep forty minutes before the alarm went off at six and when it did so, I was jarred awake, my brain befuddled and confused, blinking in the bright light of the day as the sun streamed through my open window.

Someone sneezed.

"Gesundheit," I said, closing my eyes and snuggling back under my duvet. Just five more minutes. I'd take a shorter shower and still be able to help Charity and Florence with breakfast for our guests.

Another sneeze.

I opened one eye and stared down the length of my quilt to where Mr Hoo had perched on the bedstead.

"Was that you?" I asked. He blinked at me. "Do owls even sneeze?"

As if in answer he sneezed again. A cute little headshake as he closed his eyes.

I opened my other eye and sat up in alarm. "Are you sick?"

He sneezed again and I looked at my open window and Speckled Wood beyond. Mr Hoo liked to spend a good portion of the night hunting in the wood. He'd have been out there, among all that toxicity, hunting down and feeding off small rodents, that in turn ate the insects and the fruit and berries spawned by the trees and bushes in the wood, each of which was fed by the water from the springs. We're all part of a food chain after all.

I clamped my hand to my mouth to stifle my cry of anguish.

If Mr Hoo was sick I needed help fast.

Millicent responded to my early morning phone call as I knew she would. Already up with Jasper and Sunny, she arrived at the inn before seven and ran straight up to my room to take a look at Mr Hoo.

"I'm no vet," she said as she gently handled him. "But he does seem a little lacklustre and yes, that sneeze is a worry."

"Can you create something that will help him? A tincture?"

Millicent gently patted my arm. "You know I'll do my best. It would help if I had some clue as to what I'm dealing with. Is it owl flu? Or is it some sort of poisoning?"

I clasped my head with both hands. "My money is on the latter." I filled her in on what I'd found out in the woods the previous evening. "I'm going back out there as soon as breakfast service is over. I'm going to have a poke around in the daylight."

"Let me come with you," Millicent said but I shook my head. "I'd like you to take care of Mr Hoo. Please? He's my main priority right now."

Millicent nodded. "Well alright, but remember he's just one animal out of many. I can't create enough potion for every animal in the wood."

The enormity of what she was saying cut me to the bone. Of course she wouldn't possibly be able to do that. "What are we going to do?" I asked in despair. "It's not just the animals, it's the trees and plants and insects and pretty much the entire ecosystem."

"We'll never find one solution that will fit all," Millicent agreed, worry creasing her brow.

"There has to be a way," I said, but if Millicent didn't know who would?

Breakfast service finished at 9.30. By the time I'd helped Charity and Florence to clear up the bar area, it was an hour later. I made one final check on Mr Hoo, who had started to look increasingly sorry for himself, and then hurriedly changed into a fresh robe, collected some jars and paper bags from the kitchen and made my way outside.

The day had promised to be a warm one from the minute I'd woken up, and it hadn't disappointed. The air outside seemed positively steamy, and it was a relief to take shelter in the cooler woods.

This time I walked more slowly, eyes to the ground. I wasn't sure exactly what I was looking for, just anything out of the ordinary. Through the woods I meandered, occasionally placing a hand on the bark of a tree and listening to the life within— thousands of tiny creatures who lived on and in and below the bark—as the tree drank the water found in the earth. Each one of these ancient sentinels stretched with the tips of its branches, reaching to touch neighbours, or seeking the sun. I could feel the vibration of tiny paws as squirrels and their like scampered along the branches, jumping from tree to tree, and the tiniest touches of all manner of birds as they gently alighted from forays under the canopy, feeding off the insects flying there.

And yet the heartbeat of Speckled Wood, the solid beating I had grown so accustomed to when I had wandered here on many earlier occasions, did not feel as strong and certain as it once had. It didn't miss a beat, but perhaps that beat was not as deep and assured as it had previously been.

That was a concern.

But it was the malaise of the marshland that brought the issue home the hardest.

It could only have been a few days since I had walked here, and yet in front of me, the undergrowth that surrounded the marsh was dying back. Brown bracken hung limply, and bull rushes looked dry and tired. The long grass had turned yellow. In fact, everywhere I looked the foliage had turned limp and sad looking, and a smell of decaying vegetation permeated the air.

I turned my nose up and wafted the smell away. "That reeks."

I quietly picked my way along the path until the trees gave way to more open areas and I could stand between several stagnant pools of water and stare in dismay at the dank, green water.

Algae forms on the surface of standing water, and it may not be pleasant to look at, but it is one sign that the ecosystem is healthy. Here the algae had disappeared and been replaced with a kind of coffee-coloured oily sludge. Debris littered the bank areas of the marshes, fallen twigs and bullrushes, but also—as I poked among the litter with my toe—I could make out the tiny corpses of dozens and dozens of frogs and beetles, decaying slugs and snails, a few water rats, and to my utter dismay, a recently deceased kingfisher, the blue of its plumage shining brilliantly among the detritus.

"Oh little ones," I lamented, bending down to the bird, its eyes glaring back at me somehow accusingly. "I promise this wasn't my fault." I reached out to touch it, but something held me back. How deadly was the poison in the water? Stan and Godfrey were still in hospital. I'd heard through the grapevine that Godfrey was doing better, but worryingly it sounded like it might be touch and go with Stan.

I stared again at the water, considered dipping my fingers in as I had done before, but at that time the water had been clear, and this looked more like concentrated dishwashing detergent. I plucked one of the jars I'd brought with me from my bag, and gingerly squatted by the side of the pool, meticulously scooping up some of the dank liquid, careful not to spill it on myself.

Wishing I'd brought gloves with me, I inserted my hand into a paper bag and picked up first the kingfisher, and then in a fresh bag, several of the frogs. Finally I gathered up a jar full of earth and a jar containing dead beetles and general mulch. Finally I sealed everything.

Job done.

I was bending over my rucksack to secure the buckles when I heard a noise coming from the north of me. Something larger than a bird or a squirrel, maybe a badger or a fox. The noise came again. This time more like a heavy shuffling. I peered into the tree line, half expecting to see a deer, but there was nothing immediately obvious. I cocked my head, listening, and reaching out, using my witchy intuition to search for a clue. As soon as I met a blank wall I was on my feet, scouring the perimeter in alarm.

Something was out there, and it didn't want me to know what it was. It had blocked my tentative searching with ease.

"*Revelare!*" I demanded in a hiss, and the trees swayed this way and that, disclosing secrets and banishing shadows, but whatever had been there had melted away, well out of the reach of my magick. I glared into the trees for a little longer. How could there be anything or anyone in Speckled Wood that shouldn't be there? How had they crossed Mr Kephisto's magickal barrier?

There was a definite edge to Speckled Wood

today. Someone was using magick that appeared to counter my own far too easily. Could it be The Mori? For sure they were a profligate organisation. Were they truly invincible? I couldn't fight them on my own, and despite what Wizard Shadowmender had said, I didn't see how Millicent and Finbarr were going to be of much use by themselves.

I turned uneasily for the inn, unable to shake off the feeling that I was leaving something dark and calculating to its own devices in my precious Speckled Wood.

I didn't like it one little bit.

Monsieur Emietter and Florence were up to their necks in vegetables and steaming fish when I walked through the back door and into the kitchen.

I waved at them but didn't stop to talk. Instead, I made my way into one of the cold stores accessible only from the kitchen. There were two of these. The first was used on a daily basis to store food that didn't need to otherwise live in one of the fridges or industrial sized freezers we had. The second was only utilised as an overspill at certain times of the year—Christmas for example—or when we were hosting a large event. Today I chose the overspill room, and let myself in.

This large cool storage room was largely empty apart from some forgotten bottles of ketchup in one corner. There were slatted wooden shelves on two sides of the room and a preparation table at the far end. I dumped my rucksack on the table and with clumsy fingers—the adrenaline coursing through my body—I unbuckled the straps and delicately extracted the paper bags and the jars I'd carried home. I was just lifting the last one free when Gwyn apparated beside me, scaring me half to death, so much so that I nearly dropped the jar I was clutching. I righted it at the last second and placed it safely on the table.

"My my, you're jumpy today," she trilled. "What do you have there?" She scrutinized the contents of the packages. "Is that a dead bird?"

"A kingfisher. Yes it is."

"Why have you brought that indoors, Alfhild? And why are you hiding out in here? Brrrrr." Gwyn shivered for effect and I looked at her askance.

"Grandmama, you're a ghost. You don't feel the cold."

"I can feel the memory of it."

I was pretty sure she couldn't, but I was in no

mood to argue. "Somebody has poisoned the wood," I told her.

"The wood? Our wood? Speckled Wood?"

I nodded in affirmation.

"But that's preposterous. How?"

I shrugged. "I discovered some huge plastic sacks last night that were supposed to have contained rock-salt, but I think they were actually used to carry toxic chemicals. I found them near the spring in the north of the wood."

"And the water is poisoned?"

"Yes." I rubbed my face, trying to erase the stress. "But not just the water, Grandmama. It's impacting on everything that needs the water to survive." I indicated the bird, the frogs and the jar of beetles. "This is just a fraction of what I found out there. All the grass and reeds, the moss and bull rushes. Everything that comes into contact with the water in any way, shape or form."

"And the trees?"

"It's just a matter of time." I stared down at the corpse of the kingfisher, pitying it, sorry that I'd let the worst happen. We had to act. "Unless we can find some way to neutralise it."

Gwyn folded her arms. "Then neutralise it we must."

If only it was that easy.

"But that's not all, grandmama. I think the perimeter had been breached. I felt a presence up there in the woods. Something that shouldn't have been there."

Gwyn studied me quizzically. "But the barrier?"

"I'll check with Finbarr, but as far as I know, it's all in place."

"Have you spoken to Wizard Shadowmender?"

I nodded. "I called him using the orb last night. I've asked for help, and he said he would send some, if he can find anyone available to help us. I promised I would send these samples to him. He'll have them analysed. In the meantime we're on our own." I sorrowfully scanned the items on the bench in front of me, feeling bereft for the poor creatures who had been poisoned. "But he also suggested I should make use of those I have around me." I gingerly slid the jars to the back of the table out of harm's way and turned to my great grandmother desperately. "But Millicent, Finbarr and I do not an army make."

Gwyn's eyebrows rose. She was momentarily silent. I looked back at her in surprise. Her eyes sparked with fury, and finally she snorted in derision. I quickly worked out I'd said the wrong thing.

"At times your arrogance knows no bounds,

Alfhild," she snapped with a definite bite to her words. "You are not the only witch inhabiting this inn, far from it."

Of course. People were always telling me what an amazing witch my great grandmother had been in her day. But now she was a ghost and—

"I'm not just a ghost, Alfhild. I'm a witch. Just because I'm dead doesn't mean I'm incapable of doing magick. I have the same skills now that I ever had before."

Of course she had. Hadn't I witnessed that first-hand the previous evening? At the meeting the night before, Gwyn had blown open the windows in the village hall. She'd caused quite a stir.

I could only apologise. "I'm so sorry, Grand-mama, I shouldn't have underestimated you. That was wrong of me."

"Let's not forget you have Silvanus staying right here at Whittle Inn too."

There was no doubting the power of Silvan's magick. I'd discounted him because he was a witch-for-hire with dubious loyalty. Maybe he wouldn't want to stick around. "You're right."

I realised with a fresh sense of optimism that things weren't as bleak as they looked. Silvan, Gwyn, Millicent, Finbarr and me. Then anyone else Wizard

Shadowmender could send us. "We could call on Mara too." Mara was the old witch who lived deep in the forest north of Whittlecombe. She had been a member of the Council of Elders at one time, so there could be no denying she knew her stuff.

"And don't forget Charity," Gwyn said.

"Charity is not a witch," I said firmly.

"Says who?"

"Surely I'd know?" I replied pointedly, but part of me wasn't so sure. *Yeah. The way I'd known that Jed was a warlock.*

But even as I protested on Charity's behalf I knew that Gwyn was right, and I was wrong again. Millicent had called on Charity to help her with a spell at Halloween. Because Millicent knew. And on the day I'd invited Charity to work with me at Whittle Inn, hadn't Charity told me about her experiences with ghosts? She had never struggled to see or converse with any of the ghosts who inhabited the inn.

"You do know," Gwyn replied, smug in the knowledge. "It's Charity who doesn't know. And possibly Charity's mother. But Charity's grandmother was most certainly a witch, and her great grandmother Isabella. She was one of my dearest friends."

I gaped at Gwyn is surprise. You learn something new every day.

"You'll catch flies unless you close your mouth, my dear," Gwyn told me in her brusque manner, but I could tell she was as pleased as punch to have put me in my place.

Seven of us. Seven is a good number. It has magickal properties.

But Gwyn didn't want to stop there. "It's time to call upon your father too, and the Circle of Querkus."

My father Erik had been absent from the inn for six months. His business with the Circle of Querkus, a top-secret agency dedicated to fighting back against The Mori whenever they appeared had been keeping him busy. I never had a clue where his missions took him, but Gwyn was right. The Mori were beginning to appear more frequently, firstly in October and then again at Easter, and this demonstrated how emboldened they were feeling. My own abduction, and the heart-breaking disappearance of George were tragic enough, but the poisoning of the land was a step too far.

At the very least the Circle of Querkus could support us with strength in numbers, and they'd be able to keep watch among the trees in Speckled Wood.

"How do we call them back to Whittlecombe?" I mused.

"Leave that to me," Gwyn said. "In the meantime, I have something far more pressing that I need you to do. I'd do it myself, but one of the drawbacks of being a ghost is being unable to interact with your physical world. I'll just have to entrust this task to you."

I frowned. "You make it sound as though I'm not up to it, Grandmama."

Gwyn pursed her lips. "I'm not sure you are."

CHAPTER NINE

"I can't believe you've talked me into doing this," I muttered, as I slipped out of my clothes. The prickly scattering of pine needles scratched at the sensitive skin on the bottom of my feet. The full moon floated high in the sky and the stars winked down at us, visible in this clearing in the centre of Speckled Wood.

Gwyn had brought me out here—the same pool of water where I had walked with Wizard Shadowmender just over a week ago—to meet with someone she said could help us. But for some reason the meeting had to be at midnight and the fuller the moon the better.

Gwyn had ensured I'd come equipped with a velvet pouch full of moon-bathed stones. An aqua aura quartz stone to ensure I was able to communicate with the creature I was about to encounter, aquamarine to grant me courage—something I certainly needed—and a large egg-sized moonstone to enhance my intuition and strengthen my soul.

I had a feeling my great grandmother was trying to tell me something.

When she'd informed me she had a mission for me, I'd imagined I'd need to get in touch with someone and ask them to come to Whittle Inn as soon as possible. Someone along the lines of Perdita Pugh perhaps, but a chemist rather than a ghost whisperer.

Not so.

It turned out I had to wade into this stagnant body of toxic water, armed only with a handful of semi-precious stones, and speak to someone named Vance.

Not only that, I had to do it naked.

"Could you at least look away?" I asked Gwyn as she watched me disrobe.

Gwyn rolled her eyes. "It's not like I've never seen you naked before, Alfhild. Besides, many witches prefer to undertake magick by the full moon completely sky clad.

I knew that. "I'm not a fan." I pouted. "Not in company anyway."

"Tsk tsk," Gwyn waved her hands at me. "I'm

not company. I'm family. Let's get on with it, shall we?"

I divested myself of my undergarments and thanked the goddess that it was such a warm evening. I felt oddly vulnerable to completely bare myself this way, when only hours before I'd sensed someone watching me. Were they still out there? Were they watching us now?

Well so be it.

"Run this by me once more," I instructed my great grandmother. "I wade into the water and I offer the stones?"

"You have to go right into the centre where the water is deepest and then duck under. No short cuts."

A baptism in toxic pond water. What fun.

Strictly speaking this was not a pond but a small lake, perhaps a creek might be a fitting label for it. It was fed from the stream running down the hill from the spring, and in turn it spilled out and down the valley heading towards the inn, so this wasn't the standing water you'd expect with a pond.

"How deep is it?" I wondered aloud.

"You'll soon find out." Gwyn's crisp retort did not fill me with confidence.

I retrieved a scrunchie from the pocket of my

robe and tied my hair up on top of my head, Samurai style, then picked up the pouch and hesitated. Turning to face Gwyn I asked, "Do I just offer the pouch?"

"No. Take the stones and leave the pouch behind."

I scootched to the edge of the water, trying to ignore the prickly nature of pine cones and small twigs that littered the edge of the pool, and worse—squidgy things underfoot that did not bear thinking about for too long. With one final glance back at Gwyn, who nodded encouragingly, I manoeuvred across the rocks and stepped down into the water. By night it was difficult to see just how murky and corrupt the water had become, but my active imagination filled in the blanks.

The water was deeper than expected. I gasped with the shock of the cold as my leg disappeared up to my knee, and my foot sunk into sandy silt. Off balance, I steadied myself by waving my arms about, nearly dropping the stones into the water. Before I could think about what I was doing—and therefore stop doing it—I committed, quickly plunging my other leg in. Then, grimacing with discomfort, I hobbled forwards, wary of unseen sharp objects or other dead creatures. Surprisingly the water was soon up to my hips, and another few steps had it up to my chest. I wasn't anywhere near the centre of the pool yet.

I paused, took time to breathe properly and take in my surroundings. I could see the trees beyond, and the undergrowth, but anything further away remained completely in shadow. However the moon was bright enough to light up the surface of the pond and the surrounding rocks, and I didn't need to see the rotting vegetation to know it was there.

The water, once you were used to it, did not seem so cold, but it reacted with my skin, fizzing slightly and giving me goose pimples. I dipped the hand not carrying the stones into the water, held it there for a moment and then lifted it out examining my skin, pale in the moonlight, for signs of a reaction.

Nothing. Not even a blush of colour.

"What now?" I called back to Gwyn.

She hovered at the water's edge, watching my progress. "Step into the circle of the moon, Alfhild," she called, and I frowned. What could she mean?

But as the water settled I saw exactly what she meant. The reflection of the moon, sparkled on the surface of the water. It took the form of a large white saucer, glowing supernaturally about ten feet or so in front of me. I took another few faltering steps and the water came up to my chin. It was time to sink or swim.

And so I swam. A kind of clumsy one-armed doggy paddle. Unimaginable things, probably pond weed, grabbed at my legs, but I clenched my teeth and continued. I could imagine Gwyn snorting with merriment from her vantage point, but it wasn't easy to make headway with the heavy stones in my right hand. I tried to make as little splash as possible to avoid the water rippling too much. As soon as I created waves, the reflection of the moon disappeared.

Finally I made it to where I imagined the centre of the moon would be, gently treading water, trying hard not to displace too much water or cause too many ripples. Eventually the water stilled around me and I could edge incrementally sideways.

"That's it!" Gwyn called.

"Alright," I said. I had to be crazy. What was this batty old ghost getting me into?

"Remember! One deep breath and dive down to the bottom. Leave the stones there. Then come straight back to the surface."

"Okay!" I repeated. What did she think I was going to do? Dive down and stay there? Take tea with Nautilus? Hire a submarine? Of course I was coming straight up again.

I took a deep breath and lifted my knees to my chest, sinking a few feet and then twisting around in the water so I could dive to the bottom. Scarily, in the pitch black, the bottom seemed a long way away. Finally my free hand touched the bottom, finding silt, and something harder, curved, like tree roots. Hoping I hadn't strayed too far from the centre of the pool, I fumbled with the stones, and placed them in among the roots, then I kicked off from the bottom and headed for the surface.

Going up seemed harder than coming down. I struck hard for the surface as things made a grab for me. The sensation of old sheets entangling themselves around my limbs caused me a moment of panic. I'd been underwater for far longer than I'd anticipated, and I flashbacked to the memory of my dunking in Whittlecombe's village pond and all the terror I'd experienced at the time.

Lungs burning, I kicked harder, hands stretched out, reaching for the moon. At least this time I didn't have anything weighing me down. With a supreme effort I broke through the skin of the water, inhaling air in a loud gulp.

Gasping, I turned about in the water, flailing in

the circle of the moon's reflection, wondering what would happen next. I could hear Gwyn incanting some ritual as I swam towards her but couldn't make out the words until I approached the edge. Here I could stand again. I trudged through the silt and whatever else made up the floor of the pool, plucking long lengths of slimy pond weed off my body in disgust.

"We ask that you accept our offerings and rise to hear our plea. In the name of Nerthus, and The Nix, of Belisama and Nymue, I call you from the depths of your slumber. I ask that you grant us an audience. I beg you to hear me, Vance, Keeper of the Marsh, as you heard me once before." Gwyn held her hands out to the reflection of the moon in the pool, the ripples I'd created disturbing the surface.

Nothing happened.

As gently as I could—in order not to disturb the water anymore I tried to climb onto the bank.

"Be still, Alfhild," Gwyn scolded, and I sighed dramatically. Whomever 'Vance' was, he clearly wasn't listening, or he wasn't taking the bait.

She pulled at the air, an almost comical action you might have seen in a silent movie back in her day, as though luring something out of the water. I watched her for a moment, glanced back over my shoulder... to see nothing at all... and instead concentrated on climbing out of the water.

The sides of the pool were slippery, so I grabbed onto a jagged rock and tried to haul myself up, but the water seemed to have a tight grip and held me back. For one second I had the crazy thought that something wanted to yank me back into the water.

When that pull became even more imperative, I realised I couldn't ignore that notion. I *was* being dragged backwards. Clinging to the rock to steady myself, I turned sideways in alarm, just as something erupted from the centre of the pool with an almighty splash. A wall of water ricocheted over me, knocking me backwards off my feet, where I collided slightly painfully with the rock.

With some difficulty I regained my balance and faced a being unlike any I'd ever seen before.

Imagine an oak tree, submerged beneath the surface of the water for a hundred or two hundred years, and yet oddly still living. This one was devoid of leaves, but its branches, gaily hung with pond weed instead of foliage, twisted high into the sky above my head. Water cascaded down on me as it shook its branches and I sheltered my head and stared open mouthed as this... creature... turned to face myself and Gwyn.

"Good evening to you, dear Vance." My grand-mama addressed the entity before us with familiarity and affection.

The bark of the tree split apart and a pair of sickly yellow eyes squinted at us, blinking rapidly as though in need of spectacles. From deep within the trunk of the tree came a rumble that turned to a gurgle. The tree belched and spewed forth a torrent of foul water.

"Ewww!" I screeched and scooted backwards in the water. The sudden activity gave me the strength I needed, and I scrambled up the rocks like a squirrel up a tree.

"Oh I do beg your pardon," said the tree, in a thickly sonorous voice. "I'm not feeling too well. Better out than in, I suppose." He squinted our way again. "Is that you, Alfhild?"

"Yes," I answered, surprised that he knew my name.

"It is," said Gwyn at the same time and I realised he'd been referring to her. The other Alfhild. "It's been a long time, old friend."

"It has." The tree shifted in the water, sending a tsunami over the edge of the pond. I gaped at this incredible being. I had never seen anything remotely like him, although I'd heard about Ents of course. I think I'd just always assumed they were mythical creatures that certain witches worked with and the rest of us didn't. "You look different somehow," he told my great grandmother.

Gwyn floated alongside me. "I passed, Vance. This is my spirit form."

"Indeed? And you so young? Congratulations!" This news seemed oddly pleasing to the ancient creature in front of me. "May your new guise be long and blessed."

"Thank you, kind sir." Gwyn smiled happily and indicated me. "This is the new owner of Whittle Inn. My great granddaughter, also called Alfhild, although she seems to prefer Alf, for some reason."

The tree chortled, the sound reverberating into the woods around us. "Young people today, eh?"

"Alfhild, this is Vance. He is the old man of the marsh. He's lived in this forest for hundreds and hundreds of years. He was sown from an acorn scattered by The Great Devon Oak, north of here, the largest oak tree that ever grew in the region."

"Pleased to meet you, Vance." I debated informing him that I'd never spoken to a tree before but decided that made me sound too much like an amateur. Instead, shivering in the cool breeze, I turned to Gwyn and whispered, "What does the old man of the marsh do?"

"He's a custodian of the wood, specifically the water-filled areas. The springs, the ponds, the creeks, the river nearby."

"I see." I nodded at Vance respectfully, wondering what Gwyn was planning, while simultaneously hoping he could help us.

Vance coughed. Liquid gurgling in his throat, his trunk squeezing in and out. It looked painful. "It's been a few years since you called on me, Alfhild. What brings you here this time?"

"You're sick," Gwyn said, her voice matter-of-fact. "All of the water-ways around these parts are sick. Alf here has been investigating and she thinks there has been a deliberate act of poisoning. We need your help."

I took a seat on the rocks, wrapping my arms around my chest for both warmth and decency's sake, while dabbling my feet in the water, staring up at Vance. He regarded me with hooded yellow eyes. "Can you help us?" I asked. "Is that possible? If we can't figure out a way to clean the water, the whole of Speckled Wood and everything that lives in it will die."

"And it's not just Speckled Wood," Gwyn added.

"The problem caused by the quality of the water extends down the valley, at least as far as Whittle Folly and probably beyond."

The branches above Vance's head drooped. "I knew there'd been an issue, but I wasn't aware how desperate it had become." He dropped his voice and leaned closer to us, his branches rustling above my head. "There were people here, a week or so ago. I lose track of time."

"Who were they? Did you see them?" I scowled into the woods, angry once again that our magickal perimeter appeared to have failed. How could that be?

"The same as before. The red ones."

The Mori.

"You saw them before?" I asked. "During the battle?"

"I did. And Erik spoke to me about them. Said I should be watchful." My father had known about Vance then. I wondered how many amazing beings lived in the woods that I had no knowledge of. I recalled how Gwyn had chided me when I'd considered cutting back the number of ghosts that lived in the inn. She'd informed me, in no uncertain terms, that I had responsibilities and that I was wrong to think of the inn and the grounds as 'mine'.

Now I was beginning to get a clearer understanding of what she meant.

My wonky inn was at the heart of something amazing and magickal. All the more reason to protect it.

"I haven't seen Erik since then, but I've been feeling properly grim recently so I've kept to the deep water as far as possible."

"That's not going to help you this time, Vance," Gwyn said. "We need a way to clean the water."

"Is there anything we can add to the chemicals to neutralise them?" I pondered aloud, but Vance pulled himself upright in indignation.

"You can't add anything else to the water! What has been added needs to be taken away. That's the only possible course of action."

Beside me, Gwyn smirked and held her hands out to appease the tree. "Forgive her. She's young. They believe that their modern science is the answer to everything."

"Most of the time it just makes things worse." Vance frowned, then engaged in another coughing fit, just to drive the point home.

I surrendered. "Okay, no more chemicals. So what then?"

Vance jiggled his branches, almost merrily. "Why magick of course, young lady. Magick!"

What else? I grimaced, hoping they weren't intending to rely solely on me to perform this magick.

As usual, Gwyn was ahead of my thinking. "Remember what we spoke about earlier, Alfhild."

"I'm not the only witch in the vicinity, Grandmama," I repeated dutifully.

"Far from it," trumpeted Vance. "This will be like the old days."

Gwyn nodded in satisfaction. "We'll have our own coven."

"We'll need it," Vance boomed.

The night was turning much cooler. I could see my breath as I exhaled, little clouds of steam dissipating like an early morning mist. Quivering in the chill, my skin erupting in goosepimples, I extracted my feet from the water and stood on the bank. Now we had come to the crux of the matter. "Tell me what I need to do."

I listened as Vance outlined what he needed, and my heart sank.

He had a complicated list, not much more than a riddle, and it was going to take a lot of thought on my part.

"I'll return as soon as I can," I promised Vance and he nodded, the branches above us sashaying noisily. I watched as he lifted them straight up to the sky. They whipped through the air, and ferociously twisted about themselves, like a corkscrew. Then without further ado he sank like a stone into the depths of the murky water. In seconds, every trace of him had vanished. I watched as violent waves diminished, eventually becoming gentle ripples, until the surface had settled, and the huge circle of the moon took the old tree's place.

"Come," said Gwyn behind me. "You should get some rest."

"I want to check on Mr Hoo," I said, the remembrance of his illness causing me a stab of anxiety.

I reached for my robes and pulled them on.

"Remind me again. Why did I have to do this naked?" I asked Gwyn as she floated down the path ahead of me.

"I thought it would be fun," she called back, and apparated away, leaving alone in the darkness with my mouth open.

CHAPTER TEN

I hung over the window sill breathing the summer air and listening to Zephaniah mowing the lawn somewhere out of my sight. I recalled fondly the previous summer when the ghosts had played endless games of cricket and croquet while I tried to get the inn ship-shape and ready to open. Back then Erik had been a fixture, but now my father was nowhere to be seen. Presumably the Circle of Querkus were busy fighting The Mori, one battle at a time.

I couldn't decide what to do with myself and my stomach churned with the paralysis of indecision. There were so many things for me to think about, so many different strands to my life, it was hard to know where to turn to next or whom to call on. I had to create some priorities. But what? And how? Every time I half-decided on a course of action I was reminded of the importance of something else. Round and around in circles went my thoughts, and my brain ached.

I returned to my desk and shifted a leaning pile of papers, from where they balanced precariously next to my printer, to the floor. Then I pulled a blank sheet of paper from the printer's drawer and placed it in front of me, staring at it vacantly and waiting for it to speak to me.

Needless to say it didn't.

I grabbed a pen and drew a circle. Water, I wrote.

In another circle I wrote down George's name.

The Mori went into a third circle, and finally Astutus into a fourth.

I linked Astutus to The Mori, and then George and the water to The Mori too.

All roads lead to Rome, so they say.

Rummaging in a drawer of the desk I found a neon orange highlighter. The water issue had to be the priority, but I couldn't afford to take my eye off the ball with the others.

Particularly George. He could be languishing somewhere, hurt, or worse. If he was being held he would be waiting for me, or his colleagues, or some-body... anybody to come to his rescue. The other issues were a distraction, but if I didn't do as Vance had requested the previous evening, I ran the risk of allowing Speckled Wood to die. That could not be allowed to happen.

From George's circle I drew a line and wrote down Silvan's name. I had to continue to keep up my lessons with him. I had to become more powerful, whatever it took to achieve that. It occurred to me that it might be worth taking Silvan with me to Piddlecombe Farm. Perhaps he would have the wherewithal to uncover any traces of dark magick that must have been left there by The Mori. Maybe he could help me discover something new.

I wrote down 'visit Piddlecombe with S' and highlighted that.

From the water circle I drew another couple of branches and scored Vance's name, Erik's name and the word 'security'. I needed to increase the magickal security barrier around Speckled Wood and the inn. That could be a job delegated to Finbarr. I'd already seen him this morning and knew he'd be out and about this afternoon. Perhaps Mr Kephisto could help him. I added the elderly local wizard's name with a question mark next to it. I could get in touch with him.

I continued to jot down names and ideas, until

eventually I stared in frustration at the one circle that had no plan of action against it.

Astutus.

Astutus was nothing but a digital signature on Penelope Quigwell's computers. She had a team of tech wizards working on the problem, but no useful trace had been found and nothing to lead them back to The Mori.

Except I'd ascertained there was some link between Lyle Cavendish, the landlord of The Hay Loft, and Astutus. And Astutus had made at least one payment to Derek Pearce, my old tenant whom I'd found dead in Primrose Cottage in October the previous year.

I'd bet any money there would be evidence of Astutus on Lyle's computer. You can delete files, but wasn't it the case that you can't remove every trace? An expert could crack any hard drive and find the evidence I needed.

Getting my hands on the hard drive would not be easy. Who could I find, who would be canny enough, to go in and steal Lyle's computer? I'd been barred from The Hay Loft for months, so I couldn't get anywhere near the place unless I went incognito, but let's face it, my previous attempt at undercover work, when I'd been Fabulous Fenella had not been a huge success.

In fact, I'd been pretty rubbish at it.

Florence interrupted me by walking through the open door, her feather duster hovering in the air in front of her, then swishing about as she came near my desk, intent on cleaning me into extinction, no doubt.

"Florence," I growled a warning her way and she smiled merrily at me.

"Morning, Miss Alf. Another beautiful day at Whittle Inn," she sang. "Don't mind me, I'm just going to dust your rooms."

I groaned. "That's the problem, Florence. I do mind. I'm trying to concentrate here." I indicated the paper in front of me.

Florence wafted over to me, the faint scent of smouldering cotton tickling my nostrils. I wrinkled my nose, trying to stop myself sneezing. "What are you drawing?" she asked, leaning closer.

"It's not a drawing. It's a ... a ... a mind map."

"Oh a mind map," Florence repeated knowingly, but at a guess I'd say she'd never heard of one before.

"It's to help me think straight."

Florence stopped waving her feather duster around and looked at me, her face grave. "You do have a lot going on at the moment, Miss Alf. How is Mr Hoo?"

I shook my head. "No better. Millicent has taken him home and she's keeping an eye on him there for me." I sighed and wrote down Mr Hoo's name on my paper, then drew a heart around those words, wondering which circle I could link him to. It would have to be the water, wouldn't it?

I looked again at the word Astutus. It sat like an island in its own circle, awaiting a solution.

Then I glanced up at Florence again, remembering—

Remembering how she had spied on Kat for me, when I wanted information about what was happening to the bride in the run-up to the vampire wedding. And remembering how she had snuck into the mysterious Mr Wylie's room when he had stayed at the inn in March, ostensibly claiming to be some sort of travelling businessman using Whittle Inn as a base from which to meet with clients. Florence had been able to establish that he carried an empty brief-case. No businessman was he.

Fabulous Fenella had been absolutely rubbish undercover, but Florence had been wonderful.

I could send *her* to The Hay Loft.

At first glance it seemed like a genius solution. I

wrote her name on my piece of paper with a flourish and looked up at her and grinned.

"Why are you looking at me like that, Miss Alf?" My housekeeper's voice was loaded with suspicion, and the feather duster twitched nervously between us. Her control over the tools of her trade was always impressive.

I frowned. Because that would be the challenge, wouldn't it? Florence knew about dusting and laying fires and baking. She could beat a rug to within half an inch of its life. Her meringues were light and heavenly. Her hot chocolate spirited me away to magickal realms.

But she'd died in the 1880s. She didn't know the first thing about computers.

I slumped in my chair and pouted, staring at her name in the circle on the page in front of me. Florence was the only solution I had to the issue of gaining access to information about Astutus. Her circle looked lonely. It required a companion. Because she couldn't do this alone.

I needed to locate a partner in crime for her.

And I knew just where to look.

CHAPTER ELEVEN

L ocated on the Isle of Dogs in London, in the London Borough of Tower Hamlets, Canary Wharf is a huge area of commercial estate, and the main financial centre for the United Kingdom. Many of the UK's tallest building are located in these 97 acres of what has been described as 'prime and contemporary real estate'. With acres and acres of office and retail space, you can only imagine the sheer number of workers who spend their Monday to Friday inhabiting a desk in the area. Best guesstimates suggest somewhere in the region of 105,000 people.

That's a huge number.

Think of it—105,000 people going about their business. But not really *their* business. They're usually undertaking someone *else's* business, earning pennies in order to earn enough so they can pay extortionate rent for a house or flat that is over an hour's travel away from their desk. Or if they have a mortgage, they likely live two hours away.

I'd spent six months working in a bar in the area, before deciding the sheer hysteria and wide-eyed desperation of the mainly young, absurdly ambitious and power-hungry employees, was not for me. I'd headed into the West End instead, where, rather than plotting their next move in the cut throat world of finance, people liked to chill a little more. They'd kick back and forget their woes.

What I'd learned during my six months tenancy in this particular corner of the Big Smoke, was that much of that naked ambition was rendered hopeless. Occasionally the resulting despair and stress manifested itself in depression and other mental illnesses. On more than one occasion I'd received the sad news of the passing of a punter who had chosen to take matters into their own hands and end their misery.

And that sordid and distressing memory was what had brought me back to the Isle of Dogs. The one thing I'd learned well in the last twelve months was that my capacity for calling ghosts to me was endless. To that end, I was here to channel my inner Penelope Quigwell. I intended to locate my own technical wizard.

After tacking my mind map to the wall of my office, I'd roped Florence in to my plan. She'd agreed to travel with me—I'd had to swear on Charity's life that I wouldn't lose her—and thus we had ventured by train to the capital, and after that taken the tube. Florence's face was a constant source of amusement to me—her wonder as she beheld every piece of technological wizardry that the twentieth century had thrown our way. Of course she knew of motor cars, trains and tubes - but she had never ridden on them. The prevalence of electric light, the flashing information boards, the digitally operated ticket machines, sliding doors, elevators, escalators, the sheer number of people and cars—these things all excited her. And... pigeons.

Florence was entranced by the pigeons. She'd spent the whole of her short life—twenty-two years— in our little rural backwater in Devon, apart the occasional foray to the nearby towns of Abbotts Cromleigh, Durscombe or Honiton. She had never even made it as far as the city of Exeter. Whittlecombe, situated as it was in the forests of East Devon, attracted dozens and dozens of varieties of birds— everything from sparrows, blackbirds, thrushes and wrens, to owls, kingfishers, starlings and robins. Seagulls were ubiquitous, but pigeons? There were few.

Here in London they were everywhere. As we walked the short journey from the Underground station to Canada Square, Florence stopped in the middle of the road, turning around and about, as cars rushed by her, and pigeons scavenged by the kerbs, cooing and fluttering if a vehicle came too close.

"Florence!" I called to her the second time I had to stop and turn back for her. She remembered herself and hurried after me, looking behind her as she came. "Keep up, keep up," I hissed, and a woman close by stole a sly look at me—obviously new to the capital otherwise she would have ignored me completely.

"The birds, Miss Alf," she said. "They're so pretty."

"You think so?" I asked in surprise. "Most people think of pigeons as vermin, Florence."

"Oh surely not? Such a noble looking being."

"Mmm," I said doubtfully. "Nice in a pie."

"Miss Alf!" Florence began to chastise me then pulled up short, looking at the enormous buildings that filled both our visions. Skyscrapers, that even to my eye, soared impossibly tall, reaching for the heavens in the cloudless sky.

I watched Florence ogle the buildings, tipping her head right back to follow the line of each, her face a picture, but not as much as the one or two people we had met along the journey—among the many thousands we had mingled with in fact—who had recognised a ghost when they'd seen one.

That had truly been fun.

Some of them had turned pale and looked away, others had watched in silent fascination. One or two had tried to approach her, but I'd warned Florence about keeping her head down. We had a job to do, a mission, and nothing could detract from that.

"How do they make the buildings so tall?" Florence asked.

"They use cranes," I replied, and then realizing she probably wouldn't know what one of those was either, continued, "that's like a giant steel machine that can hoist heavy loads. They create scaffolding and the shell of the building using the crane and then..."

When Florence still looked puzzled, I whirled about. I could see a dozen or so cranes on the horizon and I pointed them out to her.

"They're like some kind of iron prehistoric vulture," she mused in fascination and I nodded. "But, Miss Alf." She turned to examine the buildings more critically. "Who on earth do they have cleaning all the windows?"

"I expect they hire a small army of people like you, Florence." It seemed easiest to answer that way. I wanted to get down to business and then head back to Devon as quickly as possible.

Florence regarded me with barely concealed scepticism, so I smiled innocently and walked on, hoping she'd follow.

"Miss Alf?" She trotted up behind me. "What exactly are we looking for?"

I halted once more, standing in the middle of a plaza. The architecture was clean and crisp, the ground beautifully laid out, the stainless-steel benches and concrete planters symmetrical and ultimately bland. There seemed to be no room for creativity here, no abstract thought. No warmth.

"We're looking for someone who previously worked here. Someone who gave up."

"Gave up their job?" Florence asked. "Why would we find them here then? Wouldn't they have moved on?"

I stared up at the shining edifices above me, remembering the desperately unhappy men and women who had occasionally frequented my bar. The ones who had sat alone and wept after a bottle of red wine. Those who had nothing left to give, nowhere left to turn. Those who thought they had no future ahead of them.

"Gave up everything," I said softly. "Gave up life."

Together Florence and I spent the next hour or so scouring the general area. For some strange reason, I'd imagined we would find the ghost lights of the unfortunate quickly and easily, but it rapidly became apparent that this wasn't going to be the case.

My intention had been to target Canary Wharf for a variety of reasons. I'd expected that the number of deaths on this patch of land would be few and far between and this would mean I wouldn't be inundated with ghost lights in the way I had when I visited the Tower of London for example. Secondly, I needed a very particular type of ghost. One who had the most up to date IT skills, and where better to find them than here in the financial heart of Europe?

But it looked like I'd miscalculated. I found a grand total of five ghost lights. Two of those were construction workers killed in unfortunate accidents during the building of the complex, and two of them were homeless people who'd died during the hard winter the year before. The fifth was an elderly CEO who'd had a heart attack while chowing on his lunch one sunny spring day. He was a nice guy, it transpired after a quick chat, but his IT skills were pretty basic and confined mainly to emails and excel spreadsheets. Not quite what I had in mind.

I perched on a wall, my feet and back aching with all the mindless wandering I'd been doing. Workers poured out of the buildings close by, heading for places to grab a sandwich and I began to feel increasingly disheartened.

"I got it wrong," I sighed, and Florence turned her attention back to me. She'd been watching a group of women walk past in impossibly high stiletto heels.

"I'm sorry to hear that, Miss Alf."

"I don't know what I was thinking. I don't know much about suicide, but I suppose if people are suffering with depression or some kind of mental breakdown, then they'll tend to opt for privacy at the end." I didn't like to dwell on the myriad ways people chose to end their lives. "I'd imagined all the fed-up workers threw themselves out of windows and made strawberry jam on the plaza."

"Eww." Florence shuddered.

"I know." I looked around. "Let's just be glad

that's not the case. I suppose none of the windows open in these big high-rises anyway. Health and safety and all that."

Florence thought about that. "In my day, we didn't have all that health and safety stuff that you worry about at the inn all the time. But people," she paused before whispering, "finishing themselves off," before resuming in her normal voice, "was quite rare too. Not unheard of, Miss Alf. But such things were kept very hush hush. It brought shame on the family, you know?"

I had heard that. "Thank goodness those days are past. I think people are increasingly aware now. More sympathetic to those who suffer, in whatever capacity."

Florence nodded. "I knew a fellow, a friend of my fiancé actually, who... you know? We were all very shocked."

"Oh I'm sorry to hear that." I was. However, I couldn't help asking, "How did he do it?"

"Threw himself in front of the Exeter to Paddington Express."

I winced. "Ouch."

From somewhere close by I heard the high-pitched scraping of iron against iron, and the juddering and rumble of an engine passing over a railway crossing. There was an overground line near here as well as the underground. Maybe a station. Packed full of commuters, some of them not particularly happy. If you wanted a speedy exit after a really bad day...

"You're a genius, Florence! Come on!" I took to my heels and raced towards the source of the noise.

His name was Ross Baines.

Florence squatted next to him on the tracks so she could chat with him, and I winced every time another train rattled past me, temporarily obliterating them from my view. But each time the engine had rushed past, there they would be, my smouldering housekeeper and a rather wan looking spirit in a sharp suit, clutching a battered leather briefcase.

His ghost light had been easy to spot as soon as we arrived on the platform. There were several here, but his had burned the brightest. He'd obviously only recently died. He had the bemused expression of a spirit who hasn't quite managed to get to grips with the enormity of his passing.

Florence was being gentle with him, but he had already told her to mind her own business.

I watched impatiently from the edge of the platform, hopping from foot to foot. Several people were giving me side-eye, probably thinking I intended to throw myself in front of the next arriving train myself. I unintentionally reinforced this view because I kept issuing instructions to Florence, thereby looking for all the world like I was chattering to myself, as far as any uninitiated onlookers were concerned.

I ignored the fact that any observers possibly thought I was a tree short of a forest, because it was a case of 'needs must'. I couldn't physically get down on the tracks to talk to Ross because of the trains. I had to leave it to Florence. However Ross looked properly aghast at the apparition in front of him. I guessed it was the first time this ghost had met another ghost, and he obviously wasn't quite ready for what he was seeing.

"Get out of here," Ross was saying to Florence, attempting to push her away, and Florence cast a worried glance my way.

"Let me help you up," she offered.

"I don't want to get up. I'm quite happy down here." He was a softly spoken man, blonde with some hints of salt and pepper, and blue-eyed. He must have been somewhere in his mid-forties.

"How can you be happy here?" Florence asked, bemusement all over her pretty young face. "Here is nowhere. You'll keep getting run over by trains."

At that moment another engine rattled through the station and I lost sight of them again.

When it had sped past, Ross and Florence were still in the same position.

"You're aware you're a ghost, aren't you?" Florence asked politely. I'd warned her that some people had real trouble appreciating this salient fact.

Ross glared at her, but then his face fell. He nodded sadly. "It was all over in the blink of an eye. One second. Standing on the platform. I just couldn't take any more. It got to me. The pressure. The managers. Even my colleagues." He looked around at the tracks and the platform and shook his head. "I didn't know what I was doing. I wasn't thinking straight."

"I'm sorry," Florence soothed. Ross did appear glum.

"I should have just walked away. I have all the skills I need to start afresh somewhere." He reconsidered. "Had. *Had* all the skills."

"Did you work back there?" Florence asked. I'd

briefed her on what we needed to know. "In those huge glass towers?"

Ross ran a hand through a floppy fringe and frowned. "I did. Merman, Coleville and Bach."

"Accounting?" I called across.

"Banking."

"IT?" I asked hopefully.

Ross glared at me. "Financial security, although what business—"

"Quite right," I said hurriedly and gave Florence a double thumbs up.

Florence took a deep ghostly breath and offered Ross her best coquettish smile. "We really need your help, Mr Baines."

"I'm not sure what help I can be to you. This is my new daily existence." He waved his hands around at the concrete reinforced platforms and the tracks running east and west.

"You must be so bored," Florence sympathised. "I know I was. For many years. But I found a new role. You can too. We can help you if you help us." Florence indicated me. "Or Alf can help you cross over. If that's what you want. To the world beyond."

Ross looked up at me, regarding me with fresh eyes. "She's still alive? Not a ghost like us?"

"Yes," Florence confirmed. "She's a witch."

"A witch?" He laughed in disbelief. "I've heard it all now."

"You're a ghost talking to a ghost." Florence's response was tart. "I'd say that clarifies your world view enormously."

I watched the lines on Ross's forehead wrinkle as he considered his options. "What's in the world beyond?" he asked.

"Nobody knows. Till they get there. That's a chance you have to take."

This time when he met my eyes I knew Florence had convinced him. He nodded, and then pushed himself to standing, bending down to retrieve his briefcase.

"Tell me what you want me to do," he said, and I caught my breath yet again as another train screamed past us and swallowed Florence and Ross up in its greedy mouth.

CHAPTER TWELVE

"**A** new guest?" Charity peered into the office from the doorway. Florence and Ross had their heads together over my laptop.

"I don't get it," he was saying.

Florence giggled, "You're just trying too hard."

"This is Ross," I told Charity and when he looked up I added, "Ross, this is Charity. She's the manager of Whittle Inn."

He nodded at her warily. "Hi."

"Pleased to meet you, Ross. I hope you're settling in well?"

He shrugged and sighed in frustration. "I can't quite get to grips with things. Maybe I never will."

The 'things' he was referring to were how to use his own innate spiritual energy. Ghosts could become adept over time at harnessing sources of energy to help them make things move. Florence, for example, could operate a feather duster at twenty paces. She could move physical quantities of flour and sugar, break eggs into bowls and mix everything up and turn it into cake heaven. Zephaniah could operate a broom, a leaf blower, secateurs and a lawn mower. He could polish glass, shimmy up ladders and change tyres. I'd seen the ghostly inhabitants of my wonky inn shift rooms full of furniture around, bring beds and mattresses down from the attic, change lightbulbs, and carve joints of meat.

It all seemed to be a case of mind over matter, but observing Ross's fumbling first attempts, I could tell that practice, as they say, makes perfect.

Up until now, Ross had spent his spirit existence rolling around on train tracks. He had yet to perfect the art of levitating anything. I'd roped Florence in to try and teach him the basics. Time was of the essence and I was kind of hoping they could use the laptop to practice on and get Ross up to speed with using it at the same time. After all, that's why I'd gone in search of him.

"Ross only died a few weeks ago," I explained to Charity. "He's still reeling from all the... er... changes in his life." *And death.*

"I see." Charity ambled into the room to stand

behind him and Florence and watch what they were doing.

Ross kept reaching out to the keyboard to tap the keys, but of course his fingers slipped straight through, as though the computer wasn't really there. Which it wasn't. At least not on the plane he mostly inhabited.

"Perhaps you should try sitting on your hands," Charity suggested. "I used to do that when I was a kid and I wasn't allowed to start my dinner before we'd all said grace."

"Really?" I asked. There'd been no such rules in my house, but then after my father had disappeared I'd pretty much been left to my own devices.

"Yes, my Mum used to rap my knuckles." Charity laughed. "Not hard though," she added when we all looked at her in surprise.

Ross did as Charity suggested, but his pale face rapidly turned red from trying to force the keys to move.

I smiled inwardly as Florence—who had never seen a computer herself until she began working with me—typed some gobbledegook. She'd watched me do it often enough. "There!" she said with relish. "Try again."

Charity peered closely at what Florence had

typed. "Not exactly the start of War and Peace there, Florence."

"Which war? What peace?" Our housekeeper looked confused. Russian literature had not been Florence's specialist subject by the sound of it. I shook my head and left them to it, hoping it wouldn't take too long for Ross to grasp the fundamentals and work out a way to tap the keys. I headed off in search of a mug of tea and some cake.

I spent ten minutes listening to Monsieur Emietter converse with me in a language I didn't understand while forking chocolate sponge into my mouth and nodding and saying 'ummm' whenever I thought the conversation warranted it. Finally I picked up my mug and traipsed back upstairs to my office to ask whether there'd been any progress.

This time when I flung the door open I was surprised to find a coach load of visitors. Gwyn, Zephaniah, Ned, Luppitt Smeatharpe and the rest of the Devonshire Fellows, and numerous other ghosts who inhabited the inn. They'd all come to offer their support to Ross. The room was full of excitable chatter and my belongings were zipping through the air, on different trajectories, at a rate of knots.

"It will just happen when you least expect it," Zephaniah was saying.

"Sometimes it can help to think of something else," Luppitt appeared to be confusing matters. "Everything came clear to me as soon as I started playing my lute."

"It's less about projecting outwards and more about projecting inwards," Ned chipped in.

"Why not try typing on the keyboard at the same time as you flick the light switch with your mind?" Charity enquired.

Ross sat among them looking ever more perplexed.

"Excuse me," I said, but failed to make myself heard. "Hello?" I called. "Hello!" The room fell silent and my belongings paused in mid-air. "Do you all mind?"

"Quite clearly not," Gwyn's chippy tone rang out. "We're all trying to assist this young man, Alfhild."

Seriously? "How is this assisting?" I gestured around at the items from my desk floating at head height.

I couldn't imagine any of them were solving

Ross's problem. It had to be a case of information overload for the poor chap. I scanned the faces looking back at me, searching for anyone who knew how to operate a laptop, or even a typewriter, and failed miserably. They'd all died eons ago. If only my father had been here.

I plucked my mobile phone from out of the air in front of me. "Put my things back," I scolded, then added, "and in the correct places."

As pens and notebooks, memory sticks, plants, an owl perch, a hand bag, my witch's hat and a pile of bills made their way back to where they lived, the overhead light blinked out.

I looked up at it and then out at the sea of faces.

"Don't look at me," said Zephaniah.

I glanced at Gwyn, but her face was a picture of nonchalance.

"Hmm." I reached across and flipped the light switch back on. Two seconds later the light went out again.

"Not me," murmured Luppitt and I saw the rest of the Devonshire Fellows shake their heads. I narrowed my eyes and once more reached for the light switch to flick it on. The light came on before my hand reached the wall.

"I think that was me." Ross's soft, polite voice

drifted out from among the huddle of ghosts. There was an audible air of excitement around the room, but he merely looked confused.

"Shush everyone!" I commanded, and the ghosts quietened once again. "Try again, Ross. Turn the light off when I say." I glared at everyone else. "The rest of you... sit on your hands or something!" I heard Charity snigger. "Go," I said.

A fractional pause and then the light went off.

"And on." On it went.

"By Jove, I think you've done it," Charity uttered in her best Colonel Hastings voice.

"Off!" I ordered. "On!" The lights flicked on and off as though we were hosting a Brownie Guides' game of musical statues.

I breathed a huge sigh of relief. We were finally getting somewhere. "Excellent! Now for the computer."

A few hours later you would never have imagined that Ross had been so puzzled by the simple business of moving objects and operating electronics. He could find his way around my computer with very little difficulty and kept up a steady lecture on the transparency of my passwords and the lack of security built into my systems in his well-mannered voice. He expressed horror at the security of the websites I accessed online and total dismay at the way I stored data about the inn's guests.

I considered myself well and truly chastised.

His hands hovered over the keyboard—I could only assume this was a habit he wouldn't quickly unlearn—but he had rapidly realised he could access every letter, number, symbol, back stroke and function, merely by thinking about it. All it took was a simple nudge—a simple act of telekinesis—and he could activate the magnetic switch under the keys. I stared entranced as windows containing data rolled around on my screen, maximised them minimised, some lines highlighted as he scrolled through everything in my most obvious files, working backwards until he could access data deleted by me many moons ago.

There was no doubt about it. Ross was the IT whizz I had been dreaming of.

"There!" He sat back, looking immensely pleased with himself. "I've retuned your computer and eradicated several viruses, downloaded some better protection and isolated some of your more problematic data breaches. You'll see an improvement in processing now, but you really ought to invest in better security for your data."

"I will," I said. "Thank you."

"Is that it, then?" He looked about. "Any more machines you want me to take a look at?"

"Charity has an iPad thingy," I replied doubtfully.

"I could take a look at that one next then."

I was reminded once again that ghosts do not need sleep and have inexhaustible reserves of energy. Outside the window, night had fallen and I—after a long day of travelling and training Ross—was in fact exhausted.

"Tomorrow maybe," I replied.

He looked at me and smiled. Such a soft face with such gentle curious eyes. No wonder he had been unable to thrive in his workplace. He was not someone for whom the cut and thrust of a city career would suit. "Something's bothering you," he said. "That's why you came and found me."

I waved his concern away. "Tomorrow," I repeated.

I lay in my deep bubble bath contemplating the day

I'd had, my head aching with the stress of it all. So much to think about.

Ross. How would he respond to what I would demand of him?

George. Awaiting rescue. Perhaps. The alternative did not bear thinking about.

Vance. All the requirements needed if he was to successfully cleanse the water.

The Mori. May they be forever cursed.

Silvan. I hadn't seen him today, but I needed to make time to practice with him in the morning. Something else to add to my packed schedule. I was becoming better under his tutelage, I knew it. Faster. More accurate. Less compassionate maybe.

And Mr Hoo. The absence this evening of my wise and comforting friend disturbed me. I hadn't had time to contact Millicent to see how he was doing. I could only assume that if there was bad news, she would have been in touch with me. I sent thoughts of strength and healing floating out of the window on a cloud of steam and watched as my tidings drifted in the direction of the village. I sent them speeding on their way with a whole heart full of love.

I don't know how long I'd been lying there when I became aware of Gwyn, standing by the door and watching me. The water had cooled, quite unpleasantly, and I wondered whether I'd fallen asleep, or just dipped into an exhausted stupor.

"You were miles away," Gwyn said, but there was no edge to her voice.

"I was thinking." I blinked and sat up. "I may have dozed off."

"You look tired."

"I *am* tired." There could be no surprise there. "But don't worry, I'll be firing on all cylinders in the morning."

"I know you will," Gwyn said gently. "No point in making yourself ill however."

I rose from the bath and reached for my towel. "A good night's sleep is all I need."

"Have you eaten today?" Gwyn pressed, watching me as I towelled myself off.

I considered that. "Toast. And cake."

"I'll have Florence send you something up."

I shook my head. "No, don't worry, Grandmama. Thank you. I just want to get my head down. I'll have a proper breakfast in the morning."

"And then wear yourself out with Silvan, no doubt."

I smiled. "No doubt."

I dabbed my face with a corner of the towel and

stared at my reflection, dark circles under my eyes. I blinked and turned about to face Gwyn.

"Have you given any more thought to our encounter in the woods the other night?" She meant Vance.

"Of course," I said.

"And?"

"And I will meet his requirements. But one thing at a time. In order to do Vance's bidding, I have to find George."

Gwyn wrinkled her nose. "Are you certain of that? Surely someone else would do?"

"Would they?" I asked her. "I can't think of anyone else."

We regarded each other in all seriousness.

"Love is blind, Alfhild," Gwyn picked her words with care. "Don't let it make you stupid."

CHAPTER THIRTEEN

"So what's the deal?" Ross's cool eyes appraised me as I gulped a mouthful of lukewarm coffee and mopped at my brow. I'd been up at five, and spent two hours training—without Silvan who had remained in bed—firing chunks of ice at floating tennis balls. My spells were certainly becoming more creative, and probably more deadly, but my accuracy left a great deal to be desired, much to the amusement of some of the ghosts haunting the attic and observing my strenuous efforts to destroy inanimate objects.

From seven I'd helped Charity out with breakfast, leaving Florence free to do some more work with Ross. There could be no doubt about his intelligence, he was catching on fast. Just after nine, I'd returned to my office to see him playing a game of something extremely fast-paced via an app on my phone. I plucked it out of the air with a grunt.

What is it about ghosts? Why can they never respect personal boundaries?

Glancing through my messages, I found one from Millicent. "No change, but no worse. Come down and see him if you get the chance?"

I would love to visit Mr Hoo. I felt guilty not having seen him for a few days, but I knew he was in the best place for now. He might even be safer away from Whittle Inn. I didn't seem to be able to guarantee anyone's welfare any more.

I pulled up a chair and drew my laptop towards me, just as Finbarr poked his head in.

"All quiet overnight," he nodded at me. "I'm going to get a few hours of shut-eye and then I'll go back out and check the perimeter."

"Thanks," I replied. "Have you eaten?"

Finbarr tipped a wink. He sure had the sauce of the Irish. "I'll grab a big lunch. What are your plans?"

"Today?" I pointed at Ross. "Today is all about breaking and entering."

"Ah. Good one. I'm fond of a little of that myself." He yawned. "I'll catch you later."

"Breaking and entering?" Ross asked as Finbarr

disappeared. "That's not really above board, is it? What kind of a set-up are you running here?"

I tucked my chin in my hand and regarded the laptop in front of me. Ross had tidied the display screen and now all of my icons were lined up neatly. He'd re-organised my files so that I could find everything intuitively. I thought this spoke volumes about his character, so orderly and polite.

"Are you above a little illegality?" I asked.

"I've never knowingly broken the law."

"Ever?" My incredulity was genuine. Surely we've all done something? Exceeded a speed limit, a little childhood shoplifting?

"Not knowingly." He hesitated. "The thing is, my previous employers—"

"Merman, Coleville and Bach?"

"Yes. They wanted me to engage in certain nefarious activities, and I wasn't... let's just say I wasn't open to it."

"They were putting pressure on you?"

"Unbearable pressure." We were quiet as I let that sink in. Poor man. Work must have been hell for him.

But that was before.

I turned to face him. "The thing is Ross, what I'm going to ask you to do... you're right... it's not legal and it could get me into a whole heap of trouble."

"Then why do it?" Ross asked simply. He was sitting squarely, his face composed, hands folded in his lap, watching me with bright eyes.

"I have no choice. There are people's lives at stake. The future of my inn depends on what I do, and maybe the future of the village and its inhabitants, and the very woods around us. I have absolutely no choice."

"Well I do," he said firmly, and I frowned at him.

"Your morality is to be admired, Ross. But you're forgetting something." I wagged my finger at him. "You're as dead as a smoked kipper. Probably because you chose to stick to those very principles you're so proud of." His face fell. "Now, don't get me wrong, I admire you for that, but now that you *are* dead, you don't have to stick to the rules. You can flout them. You can break the law as often as you like. At the end of the day, there is no spirit-side judge and jury. There are no ghost prisons."

My computer screen turned to black in front of me, and I nudged the mouse to wake it up again. "What I'm asking you to do, will not only save my bacon, but also that of dozens of innocents, and with any luck it will bring justice to many who have suffered at the hands of a truly evil organisation."

Ross twisted his face up. I took that as a sign he was wavering. "Why not go to the police?"

"I did," I said. "Putting aside the issue that no-one in the mundane world is going to believe a witch and her ghost buddies, my fiancé George—who is a detective sergeant with Devon and Cornwall police —is currently missing." I stabbed at the computer screen with venom although there was nothing there to actually see on the display apart from a dozen little symbols relating to my computer apps and files. "This organisation is to blame. And I'm desperate for your help."

"I'm sorry about your fiancé," Ross said, and I could see he genuinely was. "Are you asking me to break and enter? Is that right?"

He would do it. I tried to hide my jubilation. "In all senses of the word. I need you to enter a building in the early hours of tomorrow and retrieve information from a computer there. Then we need to look at the files."

I watched Ross thinking. Eventually he nodded at me. "I'm a ghost. What could go wrong? There's so little risk." He beamed from ear to ear. "Such skulduggery! I might actually enjoy this."

I mentally punched the air.

Operation 'Looking-for-a-needle-in-a-haystack' was go.

At 2.30 am I found myself hiding in a hedge in a field next to The Hay Loft. The very same field where the Psychic and Holistic Fayre had been held a few weeks previously. Given all the rain we'd had in the Spring, the ground was claggy underfoot and I was worried about leaving footprints, but for now I needed to get on with the job in hand.

Florence and Ross hovered in front of me, casting sly glances around, bigging-up their roles as super sleuths, or criminal masterminds, depending on your take on things.

"Are you both clear about what I need you to do?" I asked them in a low voice, for about the millionth time. We would probably only get one shot at this and I wanted to do it right. I glanced up at The Hay Loft. One light burned on the top floor, and a few on the middle floor, but all the lights downstairs were out. If the landlord, Lyle Cavendish, was inside, presumably he would assume that any noise he heard was one of his guests mooching about.

Ross, who would forever be dressed in his super smart and exquisitely tailored suit, folded his arms and pursed his lips. "I think we've got the message," he said.

"Everything will be fine, Miss Alf," Florence soothed. "Stop worrying." She couldn't hide the excitement in her voice.

"I can't help but be nervous," I whispered, wiping my clammy palms against my thighs.

"We're ready," Ross reiterated.

They were. As ready as they'd ever be. "Okay. Go for it." Then added as an afterthought, "Good luck!"

I watched them melt away towards the back door of The Hay Loft, where they paused for a moment. My heart thumped in my chest as I squinted through the darkness after them. *Problem?* The little red eye of the surveillance camera blinked on and I held my breath. But what kind of image could a surveillance camera possibly catch? I could see Ross and Florence because I knew they were there. Lyle did not.

After the longest second in the history of time the light blinked off again, and Ross and Florence disappeared through the door.

Now all I could do was wait.

I don't wear a watch for a variety of reasons. Primarily, given that they have fallen largely out of fashion, I hadn't possessed one since I'd been at school. I've always been horribly clumsy, so any watch I tried to wear just never managed to stay the course with me. In any case, like most younger folk these days, I preferred to use my phone to tell the time.

I hadn't brought my phone along on this particular outing, knowing that I wouldn't be able to trust it not to start emitting strange noises. I'd found out that as a rule of thumb, Alf—or Alf-as-Fenella—made a pretty poor undercover detective. What's that acronym? *Kiss.* Keep it simple stupid? Yep. That works for me.

I huddled into the hedge, absent-mindedly extracting twigs, pieces of dead leaf and caterpillar cocoons from my snagged hair. The night was warm enough, but still I shivered a little, the anticipation of what was happening inside causing an adrenaline rush.

I waited and waited, urging myself to breathe normally, scouring the rear of the inn for any activity whatsoever. The trickier part of the mission was still to come.

For now, this was just a waiting game.

It felt like hours, but finally, five or six minutes after Florence and Ross had entered The Hay Loft, I spotted ghostly movement at a small window. I hurriedly broke cover but was just as quickly yanked backwards by my hair snagging on some prickles. I jerked myself free and, bending low to the ground, ran for the window.

We had discussed in advance the best course of action. I couldn't be certain of the security system The Hay Loft had installed, but I assumed it was more state-of-the-art-technology-based than the one I used at Whittle Inn (namely magick). I had made a guess that The Hay Loft had internal cameras and possibly seals on the doors. Once the alarm had been set in the evening, if the seals were broken an alarm would go off. I could only hope that the small windows in the lavatories at the rear of the inn had been exempted from this security arrangement. After all, the windows were so tiny, not even a Dickensian urchin would have been able to squeeze through them.

But they were the perfect shape and size to pass a laptop through.

Florence appeared in front of me on the other side of the glass. The window slid silently open—thank goodness for modern double glazing, I could only imagine the squeaking and scraping noise an equivalent window at Whittle Inn would have made—and I reached up to pluck the laptop out of thin air.

It was a tighter squeeze than I'd anticipated. I had to twist the machine slightly sideways to fit it through. It clinked against the glass. A small dull noise. Surely nothing that would disturb anyone's sleep?

A light blinked on from the top floor and I froze, muscles tense, not daring to move. I stayed that way for thirty seconds until I heard Florence hiss, "There's a light on the landing, Miss Alf."

"Get out of there," I ordered, and grabbed the laptop, not caring whether anyone heard me or not. I stuffed the machine underneath my robes, then clutching it tightly, skirted the side of The Hay Loft and out onto Whittle Lane. Behind me, more lights flickered on downstairs.

Lyle would be coming after me in seconds.

I pelted along the lane, thanking my lucky stars that streetlights were not an option the council deployed around here, but even so, the moonlight was bright enough that my fleeing figure, heading in the direction of Whittle Inn would be clearly seen.

The high hedges fell away at this point, the cultivated section of the village giving way to the forest. I opened my mouth to screech in shock as a figure dressed all in black suddenly appeared in front of me, grabbed my arm and threw me sideways onto the soft ground. I didn't get a chance to finish the sound. Whomever it was threw themselves on top of me and pushed my head into the ground.

Reminded of the traumatic night I'd lay in the dirt at the edge of the village pond, I tried to fight back.

"Be very still," a familiar voice spoke low into my ear. "Your life depends upon it."

I stopped struggling and felt something soft and heavy envelop us.

We lay that way for a little while. I listened to the sound of someone running up the road, passing us quite closely, cursing, then returning more slowly. They paused somewhere near us, and walked into the trees close by, tutting, then returning the way they had come.

A few minutes later a car drove slowly by, illuminating the trees around us, and all the time, the figure on top of me pinned me down, a warning hand pressing against my shoulder, reminding me to be still and quiet.

Eventually, the pressure eased, and the figure rolled off me, allowing me to sit up, stiff with cramp.

He reached down to help me stand, throwing a voluminous cloak back over his shoulder, and smiled, dark eyes glittering grimly in the subdued light.

"Silvan!"

He held his finger to his lips, then grabbed my wrist and led me quickly and quietly up the lane to Whittle Inn.

"You followed me?" I asked Silvan once we were safely inside the kitchen. My robes were covered in dirt, burrs, dust and dead leaves.

"Of course. I would never miss an opportunity to uncover someone's secrets." He offered me a dazzling smile. He was certainly worthy of his reputation.

I glanced about uneasily, then drew the laptop out from under my robes, placing it gently on the kitchen table. Certainly we were safe here at the inn, but still... "Do you think they'll know it was me?"

He shrugged, so cavalier. It wasn't his neck on the line after all.

"They'll probably work it out, but with any luck, by then, you'll have what you need."

"I truly hope so."

Florence and Ross apparated into the kitchen alongside us. Florence regarded me with some unease, but Ross looked as happy as Silvan.

"Boy that was fun," Ross said.

"Are you alright, Miss Alf? You look a little shaky." At least Florence was concerned about my well-being

I had to confess I did feel a smidgen unnerved. Florence put the kettle on.

I plonked myself down on a bench and slumped over the kitchen table, pulling the computer towards me. My knees were a little weak. The Mori deserved everything that was coming to them, but even so, I couldn't help but feel guilty about the theft.

"Don't open that," Ross warned me.

Taken aback I looked up at him. "Why?"

The computer slid across the table towards him. "It could be booby trapped in some way. You never know. There are advanced security systems that will eradicate data in a nanosecond if the wrong person switches a machine on."

I blanched. This was all so complicated.

"Leave it to me," Ross instructed, and I nodded, relieved that I'd lucked-out when I'd found him on the tracks in London.

"Here's your tea, miss," Florence said, as a plate of biscuits and a steaming brew appeared in front of me, followed by similar refreshment for Silvan.

Silvan twisted his lip. "I'd rather have wine."

"The bar's closed," Florence responded. I smirked. I might have offered him a drink. He had rescued me from a potentially tricky situation after all.

Silvan shrugged and resorted to the tea.

"Tell me what happened while you were inside," I urged Florence, watching as Ross carefully examined the outside of the laptop for anything unusual.

"It went pretty much as you'd said it would, Miss Alf," Florence replied, wiping down the counter top. "We went in and the whole of the ground floor was in total darkness. The office door was standing open —not that it would have caused us any sort of impediment, but still—so we went in there. Ross looked around but he couldn't find evidence of any other computer equipment."

"Everything at The Hay Loft seems to have run off the one machine," Ross interjected. "They're going to miss it."

"I expect they already have," Silvan muttered.

"We pulled the strings out," Florence resumed.

"Cables," Ross said.

"There wasn't much else on the desk there. I had a poke around like you told me to."

"His printer wasn't working," Ross added. "The lights were flashing on it. I had a quick look but I think it had run out of ink."

"Everything was going smoothly until we discovered the machine didn't quite fit through the window."

"Was it the clunk that alerted him do you think?" I asked.

"I imagine so," Ross said, his fingers hovering over the lid of the laptop. I could see he was dying to open it and explore whatever lay beneath. "Until then, we hadn't heard a peep from upstairs."

"What happens now?" Florence asked.

"You did well," I said. Her work was done. Now I had to wait for Ross to perform his own special brand of technical wizardry.

We retired upstairs where Ross finally cracked open the lid of the computer and tentatively operated the button to switch the machine on. I held my breath, watching over his shoulder as the screen turned blue, then a photo of a waterfall came up on the screen.

'Welcome Lyle' it said, and I turned my nose up.

"Password protected," I groaned. Of course it would be.

"That's the minimum security you'd expect," Ross said cheerfully enough. "Leave it with me."

So I did.

I fell asleep in my chair and awoke with a start a few hours later. I'd been dreaming of enormous reptilian-type prehistoric birds, their claws tapping at the windows of my wonky inn.

I shot forwards with a gasp. It was already light outside and the birds were joyfully singing in the trees. My neck ached from the ridiculous sleeping position I'd been in. The clicking of Ross at the keyboard must have infiltrated my dreams.

"You're in," I said, blinking in surprise, allowing the turbulent dream to slip from my psyche.

"I've discovered the best part of being a ghost,"

Ross said enthusiastically, his eyes never leaving the screen. "It seems that I can harness any kinetic energy to circumvent some of the programs. And in this case I can utilise electrical pulses to operate the magnetic switches in the keys."

"Really?" I asked, clueless as to what he meant.

"Yes, but actually what I've done is find traces of the passwords used on this machine."

"How did you get past the first screen?" I would still have been stuck on stage one.

Ross snorted. "It wasn't actually enabled. The second I pressed a key, we went to the homepage." Ross looked up at me, and I could see the excitement in his eyes. "Schoolboy error!" he drawled. I smiled back, delighted at his obvious happiness. If he'd been so enamoured by life in his old job, he would still have walked among us.

"I'm currently trying to go through everything. Give me some more time and I'll let you know what I've found."

I nodded, yawned and stretched. I decided to take a shower, and then maybe a quick walk in Speckled Wood to get some air. Perhaps I could try and catch up with Finbarr. As I left the room I glanced at the mind map I'd left tacked to the wall by the door—a stark reminder of everything I needed to do.

One step at a time, I reminded myself.

Baby steps were required.

Of course my walk in Speckled Wood lured me to the body of water that Vance inhabited. I perched on the rocks, staring into the water. Was it my imagination or was the water murkier than ever? Small bubbles lay on the surface. They didn't appear natural, but more like homemade soup that has been left out in the warm for too long and gone sour. The bubbles were motionless, not forming and bursting, just sitting there in the fetid water. The stench in the woods had become distinctly unpleasant—thousands of rotting trees, dead insects, sick mammals and birds.

I threw a couple of pebbles into the water, watching them sink, wondering whether to call Vance, but what would I say to him? Everything he had needed to tell me had been shared a few nights ago. I simply had to work out a way to meet my responsibilities.

"Soon," I murmured to the pool, assuming Vance

could hear me and that he would appear if he felt the need to. "I'll be back soon."

As I swung about on the rock, intent on going further into the wood in search of Finbarr, I spied several chunks of branches that had fallen from Vance. The ancient wood had started to dry out. I picked up a large twig, about twelve inches in length, drawn to the unusual twist in its centre— virtually a spiral—and the almost copper colour of the wood. It had some flexibility but was sturdy enough.

I turned it about in my hands, running my fingers over the fine markings. "Carved by Mother Nature," I said aloud, forever entranced by the mastery of our natural world. "She could teach some carpenters a thing or two."

It seemed a shame to relinquish my newly found treasure, so I carried it with me as I strolled through the woods, walking to the very edge of the boundary, where Mr Kephisto's magickal barrier glowed fluorescent pink, violet and blue, humming quietly with its own purpose.

I'd obviously missed Finbarr. Everything seemed to be normal along the perimeter, so I turned about to retrace my steps, walking more quickly. Things to do, people to see.

Halfway back I heard the tell-tale crunch of a branch snapping up ahead of me.

I dived behind the nearest wide tree, crouched low to the ground and peered out, listening intently for any further movement. Remembering my training with Silvan, I allowed my senses to pan out by themselves, and sure enough I picked up the faint rustlings of someone heading my way. They advanced softly, movements that were almost furtive, but couldn't hide every noise of the natural environment around them, or even control their own breathing entirely.

A dark clad figure strolled into view and I rolled my eyes and stood, making myself known.

Silvan.

"Following me again?" I asked him and he chuckled.

"Perhaps you are merely pre-empting my own movements," he said. "Very good, Alfhild. I didn't sense you until we were practically on top of each other. Your defensive magick is improving."

I smiled at the compliment. I did feel like I was making great strides. I couldn't know whether it was enough yet.

Silvan pointed at the large twisted twig sitting comfortably in my hand. I hadn't noticed I'd automatically reverted to the attack posture he had drummed into me. I held the length of wood out, aiming it at him. "I think I've found myself a wand," I said in surprise.

Later, after I had painstakingly cleaned it up, and applied a thin layer of protective polish, we put it to use for the first time. In the attic, I shot down tennis ball after tennis ball from where they darted among the rafters. Silvan had been right. Utilising a wand made my aim deadly accurate.

"I think you're really getting there," Silvan announced, and for once, it was me and not him who smiled through grim eyes.

CHAPTER FOURTEEN

"So I think I may have some of what you want," Ross was saying.

I pulled my chair alongside him to get a better look at what he was doing. Fingers hovering over the keys, he pulled up files faster than I could possibly read them, then minimized window after window.

"Tell me," I instructed him.

"Well as you surmised, the files here are buried deep and there's quite a lot of security—but what's odd is that it's only on certain things. I can access Lyle's personal material, his internet search history, his banking information very easily... and the data he holds on his guests is also kept here on several spreadsheets." Ross scrolled quickly through various files and I watched as they zoomed past me. Nothing caught my eye.

"None of this is very interesting, and I'm not sure

it's pertinent to your investigation," Ross continued. He pointed at the screen. "It gets more interesting when we look at what he's stored in the Cloud. Many people make the mistake of assuming the Cloud is secure, but that's really not the case. Any hacker worthy of the name knows what they're doing. If they want to get into your material they will."

"So what can we see in there?" I asked. It all looked like double-dutch to me. I guess I'd been hoping for something with bells and whistles that screamed out at me. 'I'm what you're looking for!'

"Documents, letters, some emails. Things that have been downloaded and saved automatically. That's the beauty of many modern devices. Unless you know how to circumvent it, you're required to save when you download any attachment, image or document. On some packages it happens automatically, and you forget that you've saved stuff. There's bags of material here in the downloads file, Alf. There has to be something of use."

I nodded, my heart beginning to beat a little faster.

And now for the golden ticket question. "Astutus?"

Ross glanced at me, unable to hide his

triumphant smile, before turning his attention back to the screen.

"Yep," he replied coolly.

I was anything but calm. I emitted a groan of ecstasy. *At last!* "Tell me." I hammered on my desk impatiently.

"Alright. You have to go in through the dark web and that's anything but straightforward." He clicked a few times, windows minimized and then the screen went black. We waited a few seconds and a little rotating icon started spinning on the screen, followed rapidly by a series of password screens that Ross completed in double-quick time.

"Once you get here the levels of security start to become more prohibitive, and I have to be honest, I'm a little out of my comfort zone. I'm wary of finding tripwires and crashing the system or alerting anyone to my presence."

"Tripwires?"

"You must have seen those films where a computer suddenly goes haywire and deletes all the information contained on its hard drive?"

I nodded.

"That's what I'm wary of. Maybe triggering catastrophic viruses or something similar."

"Fair enough." I nodded, chewing on my lip. He

clicked a few more items, minimizing and maximising screens, clicking crosses and shutting things down. Faster than I could keep up.

"In my old job I had to make sure that our systems couldn't be breached, so I'm well aware of the methods universally tried out by most hackers. The thing is, of course, that they're always coming up with new ones. I'm not au fait with everything current."

"But you're sure...?"

"That I've found Astutus?" Ross nodded with satisfaction. "Oh yeah. You told me that you'd seen evidence that they had made a payment to some-one?" I had told him that. "In any case I saw the photo on your phone, the one you took of the bank statement?"

The sneaky blighter!

Ross had the grace to look a tiny bit embarrassed, but I had a feeling he wasn't particularly.

"I used that as my starting point. If Astutus have a bank account it will be traceable, you can be sure of that. I just have to look in the right place."

So he hadn't found it. I felt slightly deflated.

"Don't pull that face," Ross said in his soft voice. "Don't go giving up on me yet. The best is yet to come. Turn your printer on."

"My printer?" I asked, confused.

"I've linked this laptop up to your printer. Turn it on."

I pressed the screen on the printer. It would normally have woken up but now it remained dark and quiet.

"Oh I turned it off at the plug," Ross said, and I noticed a smug glint in his eye. I nodded, leaned over and flicked the switch above the skirting board. Then I pressed the printer's little display screen. The machine whirred and clicked into life, the way it always did when it had been switched off for a while. After a few seconds it calmed down, waiting for a print job, but almost instantly started up again, spewing reams of paper at me.

"There was a backlog waiting on this machine. Lyle must have run out of ink but had forgotten to cancel the print jobs. I wanted to hang on until you were here to print this stuff out. I've a vague idea of what we're going to see…"

He tailed off as I rounded on the printer in excitement and snatched up a handful of pages, flicking through them, hardly daring to hope. There were invoices, copies of bills to hand over to customers. I tossed them aside, staring hungrily at the printer as it produced more information.

And this time, there it was.

A single sheet with the Astutus logo at the top. A letter addressed to Lyle, instructing him to purchase huge quantities of three different chemicals, to charge the company for the purchases, and then find safe places to store the goods.

I rocked back on my heels.

Surely this was the definite proof I needed that Astutus were behind the poisoning of the water in Whittlecombe.

"Ross," I said, waving the paper at him. "Is it possible to get a date from this? Why would Lyle have only tried to print this out recently? Is there a paper trail?" I was babbling and Ross was frowning at me. I took a deep breath. "What I need from you next is proof of a link between a gentleman named Derek Pearce, and Lyle or Astutus. Can you find that for me?"

Ross nodded slowly. "Derek Pearce? I'm sure I've seen that name somewhere."

"Where?" I demanded. "Think!"

Ross's ghostly fingers were a blur. "Oh where was it? Wait a minute."

I jiggled impatiently watching Ross work. He shook his head in frustration, tutted a few times and swore once, his forehead creased, but eventually he roared. "Got it!" I dashed to his side as he pulled up Lyle's email. Buried in the trash folder, a sent email from months before, requesting payment to Derek Pearce for 'holding goods.'

"That has to be it." I breathed out in a rush.

There would be more and Ross would help us find it, but I had listened to his concerns and we couldn't go it alone from here.

I reached for the Bakelite telephone on my desk and dialled a number.

Hundreds of miles away, a similar phone was ringing in an office on Celestial Street. I imagined a thin hand with perfectly manicured nails reaching to answer it.

"Quigwell," she said.

"Penelope," I gushed, struggling to catch my breath. "You have to get down here with one of your technical wizards. I've got some data that will be of huge interest to you."

Within hours Penelope Quigwell and three of her technical wizards had arrived in Whittlecombe and made my office their own. I couldn't move for computers, printers, scanners, a portable and secure server and the goddess only knows what else. After stubbing my toe—painfully—for the third time on the hardware littering my floor, I opted to leave them all to it.

They hardly noticed my departure, however. Whatever Ross was discovering on the hard drive of Lyle's computer would keep them all engrossed for hours if not days. I could also see, straight off, that Penelope was very taken with Ross's abilities. He was in safe hands.

As I stalked out of my office in a huff—wishing I'd set Ross up in The Nook or The Snug downstairs, the way I had Perdita Pugh back in September—I snatched my mind map from the wall and then stood in the hall wondering where I could tack it up now. It needed to be somewhere I could see it, an *aid memoire* if you like.

A kick in the pants I preferred to call it.

Florence floated next to me, a duster close by. "Everything all right, Miss Alf?" She peered through the door at Ross, surrounded as he was by Penelope's wizards, and conversing in words that might as well have been a foreign language.

I watched them too. "Yes, everything's very good. I think we've had a breakthrough."

"Will it help you find Mr George?"

I watched the printer spewing paper. Penelope was taking no chances. She wanted physical copies of every record held on the machine, along with everything in the Cloud. She fully intended to leave no stone unturned.

"We can only hope."

I stared down at the mind map in my own hand. I couldn't solve the issue of the water in the marsh until I had found George.

That had to be the next step.

I located Silvan out the back near where the stable block had stood before The Mori had burned it to the ground. We'd cleared the area and made a makeshift seating area complete with decking and the arbour from the vampire wedding. The sky was a beautiful shiny blue and billions of insects buzzed in the hedges and trees surrounding us, birds singing happily too—they had plenty to feed on after all.

Such a stark contrast to Speckled Wood, where even the grasshoppers and frogs had fallen silent, and the birds had vacated their nests and branches, and the small mammals had fled. When I studied them from a distance, even the trees drooped quietly, pale and woebegone despite the early summer's day.

I swallowed my distress. '*Soon*', I promised again, and turned my attention to Silvan.

He had his feet up on a table and was rocking back in his chair—rather precariously—a hat covered his eyes. He could have been sunbathing, it was certainly warm enough, but he was dressed head to toe, as he always was, in a silk black shirt, black leather trousers and long black leather boots too.

"Hey," he said, without removing the hat that hid his face from me. I could imagine his eyes closed beneath and wondered what he was thinking. I guessed he had heard me coming out of the kitchen door, but I wouldn't put it past him to have sensed my arrival.

The mysteries of his magick were beyond me, and I could see why most of the witches I knew would choose not to have much to do with the likes of Silvan. The darkness of black magick can be at once alluring, but also deadly dangerous. You can never quite control it.

And I imagined that nobody had ever been able to control Silvan either.

At the heart of it, his magick was about power.

Power with a capital P. And that's what I needed right now.

"Hi." I pondered on how to broach the subject I needed to embark upon. How could I enlist Silvan's help, when all we'd contracted for prior to this was his tutelage?

It turns out I needn't have worried. He was—as usual—two steps ahead of me.

"The time has come, has it?"

I pulled up a chair and perched uncomfortably, feeling oddly nervous. "How do you mean?"

"Aren't you just about to ask me to help you find your missing love?" I could hear several shades in his tone. Irritation. Amusement. I hated him for mocking me. He still hadn't removed his hat. He could be insufferably rude at times. I held my own annoyance in check.

"You should give into it you know. All that anger." Finally he plucked the hat from his face and sat up to face me, his hair falling over his eyes which sparkled with glee. "I've told you before. Channel that anger to where it's useful."

"You have mentioned that before, yes," I replied. "Repeatedly." I took a deep breath, willing myself to remain calm, and placed my hands flat on the wooden table in front of me, enjoying the feeling of the wood grain under my fingertips, while allowing my feet to connect with the natural world through the earth.

"You're right. I do need your help," I announced. "I probably can't do what I want to do without it."

Silvan nodded, his face became serious for once, and when he spoke it sounded sincere. "I'm at your disposal. What's the plan?"

CHAPTER FIFTEEN

W hat's the plan, Alf?

Oh to have one.

Just after midnight, Silvan, Finbarr and I walked up the dirt track that led to Piddlecombe Farm. The scent of cow manure stank stronger than ever in the fields around us. The evening was fine and dry. Slow-moving clouds occasionally blotted out the light of the moon, but on the whole we could see reasonably well. Unfortunately that meant there was a possibility we would also be seen.

All of us had dressed in dark clothing and boots of course, and we stuck closely to the tall hedges on either side of the dirt lane. Silvan, always alert, had his wand drawn, ready for anything unexpected. Finbarr too remained wary, his hand not far from the pocket where he kept his. I occasionally reached into the pocket of my own robe to feel the chunky twig I'd requisitioned. I still couldn't think of it as a wand, but the more I touched it, the more comfortable it felt in my hand.

Over the past few weeks I'd searched high and low, and queried everyone I could think of who might have some inkling of the whereabouts of George. I'd used the orb. I'd plagued Wizard Shadowmender and Mr Kephisto. I'd consulted fortune tellers and psychics whom I'd met at the Psychic Fayre, and I hadn't found the slightest trace of him.

I'd concluded that he was either dead, or The Mori had him where I couldn't find him, in some dark, secretive world to which I had no access.

If that was the case, then who better to help me find him than Silvan?

Ignorance is not bliss. It is a deep black well. You cannot cast light on things you don't know exist. But Silvan did know of the existence of many dark things. Through him I intended to learn more—so much more—about magick than I ever had before. So the plan—such as it was—meant starting right back at the beginning, at the moment in time when George had disappeared. The memory of the phone call, when George had sounded alone and desperate, remained fresh in my mind. He'd come to Piddlecombe Farm because this is where I'd sent him, but he should never have come alone.

This was where I'd heard from him for the final time, and now I was hoping that Silvan, a master of the dark arts and a necromancer, would be able to help me find something, some bare trace of George's existence.

We crept quietly along, my feet sinking into the softer mud at the edge of the track where the sun didn't quite reach to dry it out during the day. We moved slowly and cautiously, ears and eyes straining to catch the sights and sounds of anything untoward, senses primed to pick up anyone heading our way.

After half a mile or so, we spotted a white sodium light shining brightly out into the night. As we moved closer, I could see how it lit up the entrance to the barn on the left and illuminated the other buildings around it.

We passed a long row of tall storage units on both sides of the track and made our way closer to the main buildings, staying out of the circle of light as we headed into the danger zone. From somewhere, one of the outbuildings possibly, or the farmhouse itself, a dog barked a sharp warning. Once, twice.

Silvan raised his wand. "*Somnum penitus.*" The barking ceased abruptly. We remained where we were, and I looked around uneasily. Where did The Mori sleep at night? Did they even need to sleep? Were they watching us now?

Silvan held his hand up – a signal to bide a while longer. We remained in place for more time than one might imagine necessary. If anyone had been alerted by the dog barking they would be watching. They would continue to watch far longer than the average person would wait. But Silvan wasn't the average person. He elected to play a waiting game. We stood behind him, listening to the lowing of cattle in the barn, and the stamping of hoofs as the beasts shifted about, waiting for the early dawn and the arrival of the farm's manager who would let them out into the fields and later bring them in again for milking.

Finbarr had been keeping a watch on the farm from time to time over the past few months, spending hours camping out at a safe distance with a pair of binoculars. He'd observed the comings and goings of personnel. Our best guess was that one or two henchmen occasionally stayed in the farmhouse itself, but certainly not every night. The farm appeared to be run by a manager and a few agricultural workers. The only animals on the farm were the small herd of cows and occasionally someone's German Shepherd dog. No chickens, no pigs, nothing else. None of the surrounding fields were worked. Fields further away from the main building had been leased to other farmers or smallholders, and many outbuildings were under-utilised or simply remained empty.

The main income for the farm appeared to be from the storage units, now behind us. Here, people such as Rob Parker, of Parker's Porky Perfection fame, stored his sausage wagons. Finbarr had checked the units out and found an array of interesting contents—everything from some classic 1950s sports cars, several tractors, and a unit full of dolls' heads—absurdly spooky. Someone even appeared to be storing tinned food in case of a forthcoming apocalypse. But, really, it had all been fairly innocent.

The buildings we were most interested in were the farmhouse itself at the top of the lane and the row of smaller storage buildings to our right. Now that I saw them again, I knew this was where I'd been held on the night of my abduction from the Fayre. I recognised the cow barn and the farmhouse, and the large muddy expanse of ground between the three key areas.

A filthy Land rover, the number plates obscured by mud and the windows thick with dust, had been parked on the verge, close to the hedge. Finbarr, always light on his feet, scampered over, and peered inside. He tried the doors—all locked—then came back to us with a shrug.

As we began creeping forward again, I grabbed Silvan's sleeve and tugged gently to alert him to the buildings on our right. I wanted to look inside. Silvan nodded at me and cocked his head to motion me to go first. He gestured with his wand at Finbarr to position himself by the door and keep watch.

I carefully tried the heavy door, fearing it would be locked, but it swung open easily enough and I stepped inside. It smelt musty, having been closed-up for a long time—and of something else. Something with a slight chemical tang that reminded me of my time spent here. The large plastic sacks—the ones that had first alerted us to the possibility of chemicals—remained in the corner. I slipped over to them, taking out my mobile and snapping a few images of them. They matched the ones I'd found in Speckled Wood.

Silvan came inside with me, scenting the air and wrinkling his nose in distaste. He illuminated the tip of his wand, peering into the dark corners, and pointed it at the ceiling. I couldn't be certain what he was looking for, but his eyes swept this way and that, pausing to look more closely at certain objects or markings – a spider's web, scuff marks on the floor, a scratch on the wall.

When he'd done, I pointed silently at the large door built into the floor and we stood alongside it. I reached out to heft the heavy weight, recalling the loud clang it had made the last time I'd opened it and let it fall, alerting my captors to my escape. Earlier today I'd briefed Silvan about my brief stay here at Piddlecombe Farm and forewarned him of this door and the passage that ran below. It headed in the direction of Whittlecombe, eventually opening out in a natural cave south of here.

We'd agreed that unless the cave had somehow been closed off since the last time I'd been inside it, George could not be held below. Nonetheless, Silvan gestured at me to move away from the door and instead waved his wand. The heavy door laboriously rose by itself, tipped over and slipped quietly to the ground without so much as a rustle or a clink.

Silvan fell to his knees and pushed himself flat against the ground. Wriggling to the edge of the drop he peered into the hole, directing his wand into the darkness, to scrutinize all he could see, hear, sense and smell.

Finally he stood and shook his head.

Nothing to report.

George had not been held here.

That left the farmhouse.

With our backs pressed to the storage building we each inspected the late Georgian, early-Victorian farmhouse ahead of us. All the lights of the neat brick building were out, and the squat single-paned windows stared blankly back at us, giving nothing away. I couldn't spot any movement behind the filthy glass and I could hear no noise, save the restless shuffling of the cows in the barn to our left.

In order to reach the front door we would have to head through the circle of light. But that was not an option. Instead, we'd have to make our way around the back of the storage buildings and approach the farmhouse from the rear.

We doubled backed, walking in single file, Silvan taking the lead, me in the middle, Finbarr bringing up the rear. Occasionally Silvan would raise his fist, like a marine in one of those US action movies, and we'd each stop in our tracks. One of us would investigate a rustling or squeaking or other odd noise, and then when we were sure we hadn't been discovered, we would push on.

Once or twice, to my utter chagrin, I stood in an enormous soft pile of something unpleasantly fragrant and cursed the fact that we had to travel through a cow field in the dark. I shuffled along, dragging the offending foot, trying to wipe off the mess, until Finbarr gave me a little push and I had to dash to catch up with Silvan.

After we'd navigated around the back, we had to dodge through piles of outdated and rusting farm machinery, difficult with such limited visibility. The shadows were long and my eyes strained to peer here, there and everywhere all at once. Still no signs of life. It looked like nobody had been around the back of the farmhouse in donkeys' years. I huddled up close to the wall and then curled my head around to peer into the grimy window. Old net curtains, yellowed with age, obscured my view into what I assumed was the kitchen.

Silvan joined me.

"I can't see an alternative way in. No entrance through a cellar or a side door." He ducked his head to speak low into my ear.

"And I can't see any light from within the building. I say we risk it," I whispered in reply and reached out to nudge Finbarr. "Let's go in."

Silvan tapped the lock of the building with his

wand and waited, his eyes drilling through the flaking paint of the door as though searching for life beyond, otherwise unseen. After ten seconds or so, he tapped the lock again and I heard the reluctant click of dry tumblers. He placed his hand lightly against the door, and slid his wand up, "*Unlūce*." I heard a bolt draw back. He repeated the exercise at the bottom of the door and then turned the handle.

The door swung open, creaking a little and we squinted into the dark. It was a kitchen as I'd thought, although not one that had been used that way for a while. Silvan entered, illuminating his wand once more. I followed him through, drawing my own wand now, and turning in circles, reluctant to have my back to anything or anyone.

The work surfaces and kitchen table were covered in rubbish. Old take-away boxes and bags, foil trays containing leftover food, takeaway coffee cups, plastic bottles of fizzy drinks. The stink of rotting food and spoilt milk was nauseating. I tried to stop breathing in through my nose, glad that Florence and Monsieur Emietter couldn't see this.

Finbarr followed us in and quietly closed the door behind himself. He too circled in place, observing the mess.

"What do you notice?" the Irish witch whispered.

I glanced about. "Apart from the mess you mean? There doesn't appear to be anyone here. And there probably hasn't been, not for a few days at least."

"That's right. But it's not just the lack of *anyone*. There's no-*one* and *nothing* here. Not even rats."

Silvan dropped his wand to the floor and then directed it at the kitchen table. No rodent droppings on the table or even on the floor, that much was apparent despite the rubbish spread everywhere. No insects either. "I find that strange." I noted the unease in Finbarr's voice.

"Come on," I said, keen to press on with what we needed to do. "Let's keep looking."

Silvan moved out into the hallway. Ahead of us was the main entrance, with a door to the left and one to the right. A flight of stairs led up from the front door. Closest to us, there was another door under the stairs. Silvan gingerly opened the latter, and shone his wand about. A flight of rickety steps heading downwards to a cellar.

"Let's split up," Silvan suggested. "Finbarr, you take upstairs. I'll go down. Alf, you concentrate on this floor."

We murmured our agreement and Finbarr

scooted round us to take the stairs up. He and Silvan had their own source of light. I looked down at my own wand, still so humble and little used. Silvan chortled quietly and reached out with his own, tapping mine at the tip. It lit up as though a sliver of a star had lodged itself there, and then he disappeared leaving me to marvel at the wonder of his magick.

I made another circuit of the kitchen, using my wand like a torch, opening drawers and cupboard doors, but there was nothing here to see except old utensils and tins of food that according to the sell by date had been in the cupboards for five years or so. I'd bet any money that five years had been the amount of time Jed's father had been the owner of the farm.

In the cupboard below the sink I found sacks of dry dog food, musty with age. I was reminded of the dog we'd heard barking. Where did he live if not in this house? And I wondered again about the old man who had lived here. What had happened to his dog?

A loud bang from upstairs made me jump. I dropped into defence stance. A brief silence was hastily followed by a muttered curse. It sounded as though Finbarr had collided with something heavy, tipping it over. Heart racing, I moved quickly into the hall and shone my wand up the stairs. Finbarr appeared on the landing, rubbing his forehead and waving at me.

"It's fine," he said, his voice low. "Nothing to see here."

I nodded, intent on returning to my own search. I paused at the front door. Locked and latched and covered in a curtain. I pulled the curtain aside and peered through the eye hole. The sodium light lent me the ability to see a fair distance. Outside all was quiet. The only signs of life were the moths and nocturnal insects that danced under the light. The muddy ground remained just as we'd left it. The Land Rover sad and still.

I dropped the curtain and heard the tell-tale jangle of keys. Pulling the curtain back once more, I spotted several sets of car keys—or tractor keys perhaps—hanging on nails to the side of the door. Could one of these belong to the Land Rover?

With nothing to see in the kitchen I tried the door to my right. I pushed it gently open, and crept forwards into the shadows, finding myself in the living room. It was a large space, dominated by a once impressive tiled fireplace. The open grate had been removed and replaced with an electric fire, something out of the 1970s. I doubted those things were still legal. The room smelt slightly better than the kitchen—but you could tell it had been shut up for a long period of time. As I moved past the window I disturbed the heavy curtains hanging there and dust billowed into the air around me, swirling like smoke in the light from my wand.

The floor had been laid with a badly-stained burnt-orange carpet. It had been partly rolled up to reveal floorboards. The walls were covered in some equally horrendous flowered paper, orange and yellow, brown and beige. A stained mattress had been positioned in one corner and several Bentwood chairs were arranged around the fireplace, but apart from those few items and several ashtrays full to the brim with ash and butts, there was no more furniture and no further accessories.

I sifted among some of the piles of rubbish, but just as I'd found in the kitchen, they contained nothing of interest. More food wrappers, old crisp packets, empty cans and bottles of drink.

That left one more room to search.

Closing the door of the living room softly behind me, I crossed the hall again and tried the last door. This one creaked on its hinges as I opened it. I held my wand up and whistled under my breath.

Here we had an office or study of some kind and,

judging by the modern equipment, a computer, and a printer for starters, this space had been utilised more recently. The light on the printer was flashing. A fault? I remembered how Ross had managed to print out documents from Lyle's computer, so I opened the printer tray to check for paper, and sure enough it was empty.

A large modern desk had been placed in the middle of the room. It was covered in paper, letters, documents and such like. I quickly flicked through what was there and opened a couple of drawers. I found an open package of blank A4 paper, so I pulled out an inch or so, and neatly filled the stacking tray, before slamming the tray shut and waiting. The printer whirred into action—a satis-fying sound. At home, Charity was forever rescuing me when mine seemed to be perpetually jammed and refused to print for days on end. Occasionally I lost patience with it and threatened to send it flying out of the office window, to forever rest in pieces on the lawn outside.

While I waited for the printer to spool and do its thing, I had a closer look at the mass of paperwork on the desk. Much of it made no sense to me. There were numerous printouts of Excel spreadsheets with numbers on them for example. I pulled out my mobile phone and took a few random photos to show Penelope Quigwell, before searching for something more obviously interesting. I sifted through a few letters, many still residing in their envelopes.

Mainly addressed to a Mr J Bailey, the only striking thing about them was that they had been sent from all over the world. I spotted brightly coloured stamps and official-looking postmarks for Germany, France and Spain, Croatia and Russia, China, Indonesia, the USA and Columbia.

Perhaps the contents of the letters were encrypted because they read like childish greetings.

My dear JB

I hope this letter finds you and yours well.

I heard of the recent success of your trip abroad.

That was a great result. I'd be interested in planting begonias next year. Perhaps we could discuss?

Looking forward to hearing from you in the near future.

Yours respectfully

Kinver

Planting begonias? I snorted in derision. Was that some sort of code?

"You won't be planting begonias if I can help it, Mr or Ms Kinver. No way," I muttered and stuffed the letter along with a host of others inside my robes. We had agreed before we embarked on Operation Piddlecombe that we wouldn't remove anything from the premises, but given how much paper there was piled high on the desk, surely nobody would notice.

I tapped the computer keyboard and the screen lit up, password protected. Maybe we should just spirit this one away with us too. I was sure Ross would enjoy the further challenge of unlocking this one, although I had no doubt The Mori would have wised up after their recent security breach.

The printer had finished its juddering lament, so I scooped that paper up too, rolled it into a long tube, and again deposited it in a deep pocket. Feeling weighed down I slipped back into the hall. Finbarr was coming down the stairs, an egg-shaped bruise forming on his forehead.

Silvan appeared at the top of the cellar steps. "I think you should come down here," he whispered. "Come and look at this. Mind how you go."

We followed him down the rickety stairs. They sank beneath our weight as though they weren't properly fixed to the wall. Convinced they were about to collapse, my stomach lurched in fear once or twice. The staircase turned at a right angle halfway down, and at the bottom I found myself in a corridor with a small rabbit warren of rooms leading off it. Only one door stood ajar.

"I've checked them all. Most of these are storage rooms. There's some really odd stuff down here." Silvan raised his eyebrows in mock horror, and I wondered how it could be that he'd been taken by surprise by the oddities and weird things deposited here, given his own questionable background. "We should burn this place to the ground. It would be no great loss."

He walked to the end of the short corridor and pointed inside the last room, the one with the open door. Finbarr and I traipsed towards it and I entered first and waved my wand around so that I could see.

The room was boxy, maybe 12 feet square. Yet another mattress had been tossed into the corner, but this one had been covered in blankets. A bucket had been placed in one corner, and a wooden chair, a partner to the Bentwoods in the living room, took pride of place in the middle of the room, facing the makeshift bed. A jacket had been slung over the back of this chair. There were books piled up next to the mattress, alongside a tray carrying a wrapped sand-wich and a bottle of water.

The sandwich appeared quite fresh. I bent down to take a closer look. Egg and cress. The sell by date was for four days previously. I recognised the pricing ticket and the make of sandwich. This had been bought at Whittle General Stores just a few days ago!

I held the sandwich up to show Silvan. "We can't know this was George. Surely they wouldn't have kept him here this long?"

Silvan pointed at the pile of books and I reached over and picked up a handful. Lee Child, Mark Billingham, Robert Harris. Although not exclusively so, these were books men might read—and that made sense. No chick lit or romance or family sagas here. Assuming someone had bought the books for George, they would have chosen things that were universally popular. All three adorned with a bright yellow supermarket tag proclaiming 'three for a tenner'. Good deal.

I dropped them on the bed and shuffled through the other books. Similar. More yellow stickers from the same supermarket. And a puzzle book. I scanned the completed crosswords and my heart skipped a beat. This was George's handwriting, no doubt about it.

"He has been kept here, and judging by the sandwich wrapper, we've only just missed him," I said. My head and heart were heavy. *So close.*

I scrutinized the room once more. Took in the jacket over the chair. I reached for it. A light summer jacket in pale blue, with something heavy weighing down the pocket. The garment itself was far too small for George and it wouldn't have fitted me either. I held my wand to the label. A UK size 10. A woman's size.

I reached into the jacket pocket and drew out the contents—a small navy jewellery box, much like the one George had presented my engagement ring in, and a mobile phone. Same make and model as George's. I pressed the button on the side, but the battery had died, and nothing happened. Impossible to know for sure whether it was his, or whether it belonged to the mysterious woman who had left her jacket behind.

A bit of a coincidence though.

Confused, I turned about. There was only one mattress. And one sandwich and one bottle of water. That suggested to me that George had been held here alone. The woman had therefore been his captor or his guard.

So George had been held here by a woman?

A small woman would have been no challenge to him. He could have overpowered her.

Unless she had a way to keep him under control.

Which she would have, if she was a witch or a warlock.

The Mori were not known for allowing women into their ranks, although female warlocks were not themselves a rarity.

"Where can they have moved him to?" I wondered aloud.

Finbarr pulled at the blankets. "Do you think they've abandoned the farmhouse? Maybe gone in search of pastures new? Literally."

"They'd never abandon Whittlecombe," I said. "For some reason they're forging a bitter war for it."

"If we had a better understanding of why, that would certainly help us fight them. We—," Silvan started to reply, but I held my wand up and stopped him in mid-flow.

A faint buzzing sound.

Like an angry hornet.

My heart jumped into my throat. "We need to get out," I hissed urgently.

Silvan cocked his head to listen, but Finbarr understood straight away, and flung himself out of the room and into the corridor. I yanked at Silvan's arm and dragged him out with me, running for the stairs. This time I didn't let the sponginess of the wood worry me. I clumped up them as fast as possible, ignoring the sense of being unbalanced.

I turned right out of the cellar door, just in time to see something red in the corner of my vision. "Finbarr!" I shouted, "Look out!"

I heard a shriek of agony and a loud thump as Finbarr fell to the floor. Without thinking twice, I lifted my wand and hurled a ball of energy at the spinning globe in the kitchen. It retreated, taking shelter in one of the open food cupboards. We had it cornered.

I followed it in, my wand held ready to strike out at it again. Silvan, similarly armed, pushed past me and reached Finbarr who was sitting up and clutching his arm to his chest.

"We need to get out of here," Silvan said. "Finbarr. Can you stand?"

"I can," he said, but struggled to do so until Silvan reached for him and pulled him up.

With one eye on the globe, hiding its light among

the ancient tins of beans and spaghetti, I reached for the back door and yanked it open.

What I saw there had me slamming the door in double quick time. Red globes, of varying sizes, slipping out from among the piles of rubble, and rusted farm machinery. Dozens of them.

"All this time we thought we were alone, yet we've been walking through their nest," I said, retreating from the door.

"How many?" Silvan asked, calm and assured as always, his eyes sparkling with delight at the prospect of the fight ahead of us. He had been born for this.

"Too many." I spun around as the red globe in the cupboard buzzed with what sounded to my ears as smug delight. I zapped it again and it scuttled into the shadows.

"Blasted things." I looked at the front door. There were fewer places for the globes to hide out the front. We had to go that way. There was no other alternative.

"The Land Rover," I said.

Finbarr, sweating profusely in his agony, shook his head. "The doors were locked."

"But I found some keys. Come on!" I urged them to follow me and I dashed for the front door and reached for the keys hanging behind the curtain. Four sets and no straightforward way to tell which ones—if any—would belong to the Land Rover. The vehicle was so old it didn't even have electric locks.

No time to worry about that now. I grabbed them all and drew back the door chain, quickly followed by the bolts top and bottom of the door. I gripped the handle and turned back, my heart thumping in my chest.

"Are we ready?" I asked Silvan, who held Finbarr up, his wand raised and ready for action.

"Always," he replied with a dashing smile. I took that as my cue to throw open the door and launch myself out into the unknown.

Wand raised, I whirled around rapidly, blitzing anything that moved, shooting arcs of light across the sky above me, or into the shadows around me. Nothing but a handful of charred moths fell at my feet. I skidded to a halt, Silvan behind me.

"Easy," Silvan murmured. His voice cut through the adrenaline that had me on the edge. "Remember all we've practised. Stay low, stay sharp." He gave me a gentle push. "Now go."

I ran for the Land Rover, keeping my body as low as I could manage. I passed the cow barn and heard their murmurings of discontent, their feet heavy on the packed earth inside. A flash of red zipped past my ear, and I ducked quickly but kept moving, zig zagging my way towards the 4 x 4.

The air exploded around me as I reached it. It had been parked facing the farm, meaning I had to move into the open in order to try the keys in the lock of the driver's door. I fumbled with the first set as I heard the buzzing of a globe just metres behind me. A crack of Silvan's wand and the thing was sent spinning into the hedge with an angry howl.

Silvan joined me as I jabbed the key from the next set into the lock. It wouldn't even go halfway in. I pocketed that and tried the third, as once again, Silvan shot at a globe heading our way. This time the rotten thing exploded, and I felt the heat of its energy scorch my cheek. I ducked again, somewhat after the moment, and then punched the key in my hand hard into the lock. It went all the way in. A swift twist and the door opened. I jumped in. Silvan tapped on the back door. I reached behind me to unlock it and he flung it open. Then I thrust the keys into the ignition.

"Don't be a Hollywood horror movie," I muttered as I twisted the keys. The engine turned over but didn't catch.

"I said don't be a Hollywood horror movie, you son of a—"

The engine flared into life with a satisfying throaty chug, and an explosion of exhaust. "Get in, get in, get in!" I shrieked to Silvan.

Silvan practically threw Finbarr onto the back seat, then jumped in after him. Before he'd even had a chance to close the door, I'd slammed the car into reverse and was hightailing it—backwards—down the lane, the engine protesting loudly at the speed at which I was forcing it to go.

We'd had no time to pull on our seatbelts and now as the Land Rover rolled in and out of the deep potholes, we were thrown around and jolted about, but I hung onto the steering wheel for dear life, craning to look behind me so that we wouldn't end up wedged in a hedge or impaled on a wooden fence.

Silvan rolled his window down and stuck his head out, directing his wand at the stray globes that had chosen to follow us. Sparks flew as they sent missiles our way, bolts of energy hitting the body of the car.

"Keep going," Silvan called, sounding thrilled, but I didn't need his encouragement anyway.

George was still alive—and today was not my day to die.

CHAPTER SIXTEEN

I pulled the Land Rover up beside the inn and tucked it in behind Jed's van. As I climbed out I couldn't help but marvel at the collection of Mori vehicles I was beginning to accumulate.

Unfortunately, I was pretty sure I'd just broken the law by taking the vehicle and driving it without consent.

Never mind. I had more important things to worry about for now.

I burst into the inn ahead of Silvan, and then wheeled about to help him with Finbarr. We sat the Irish witch in one of the high-backed armchairs in front of the fire. The embers glowed orange, but Florence appeared as if by magick and, taking one look at Finbarr, proceeded to stoke the fire and breathe life back into it.

Gwyn was hot on her heels.

"What happened?" she asked, tapping her wand against the wall and switching the lights on, allowing us all to see a little better.

"We've been at Piddlecombe Farm," I explained hastily, "looking for signs of George. Unfortunately we ended up in an ambush."

"Our friends?" Gwyn asked and I nodded.

"Don't worry, we gave as good as we got," Silvan said gleefully, and Gwyn shot him a look that was a mixture of scepticism and approval.

"You're okay?" she asked me.

"I'm fine. It's Finbarr. He got in the way of a little one."

Gwyn drew out her wand and scanned Finbarr's arm with it. "Nasty," she said. "We'll need to get him to a hospital."

"Oh, I don't want to be doing with that, now," Finbarr protested. "Is there nothing we can't be doing ourselves, like?"

"Absolutely not," Gwyn replied sternly, then half turned away before swerving back and directing a quick zap from her wand at Finbarr's arm. He shrieked and she smiled, her eyes glinting with what can only be described as sadistic pleasure.

"Put the arm in a sling," she said to me. "That

will do for this evening. We'll get him to a doctor in the morning."

Finbarr whimpered as I crafted a makeshift sling from one of Charity's gaily coloured shawl-scarves—the first thing I could lay my hands on. He did however confess that much of the pain had disappeared thanks to the 'shot' Gwyn had given him. We left him to rest, dozing in the chair next to the now roaring fire, with Zephaniah standing guard and providing company, and disappeared into the kitchen to huddle around the big table there.

"What did you discover?" Gwyn asked.

"Gilchrist had definitely been held there. I found traces of him in several of the store rooms in the cellar, but I could feel his presence most in the end room." Silvan shrugged, his face grim. "We'd only missed them by a few days."

"I recognised his writing on some puzzle books that were left behind. Oh and we found his phone, I think." I said. Who needed necromancy? I pulled it out of one of my pockets. "It needs charging."

"But he wasn't there?" Gwyn asked.

"We didn't think anybody was there," I replied. "We were wrong." I narrowed my eyes. "There were dozens of them. I likened it to a nest at the time. I can't understand why I can't sense them."

Silvan's eyes darkened. "I've been considering that too. I think when they're in globe form, they don't seem to emit any kind of trace until you see them or hear them."

"Tricky little blighters." I breathed out hard, struggling to relax even now in the safety of the inn.

Gwyn twitched. "Nothing else?"

I knew why she was nervy. We had to find George so that I could appease Vance and cure the marshes of their malaise. I was about to apologise and answer in the negative when I remembered the letters and the paper from the printer. I drew everything out of my pockets and created a small pile on the kitchen table.

Silvan sifted through it, remarking on the stamps, and creating sub-piles according to country.

"I have no idea whether these letters will help Penelope Quigwell," I said, "but perhaps there are physical traces or clues within the content that will help her unlock access to new members of The Mori we have no prior knowledge of."

I picked up the sheath of paper that had been expelled from the printer. I was disappointed to see that many of the pages were blank, and several contained nothing but gobbledegook. However, it was in among those that I found a short email chain.

'It has come to our attention that our local agent, D Pearce, has been storing some of our products at his allotment. We fear he may be attempting to dissemble. Naturally we are concerned that the products may be discovered and lead to untoward repercussions.

Please advise.'

The response was short and sweet.

'Dispose of said agent and related evidence.

Ensure he has not attempted to contact others.'

"Derek Pearce." I clamped my hand to my mouth. "This is his death warrant."

"You said the globe you saw that day had been waiting around," Gwyn said.

I nodded. "Derek had been dead for at least twenty-four hours. It looks like The Mori were waiting to see who would try and make contact with him."

"They thought he was a double agent," Silvan remarked.

"But as far as we know, he wasn't. Nobody on our side was aware of what he was doing." I frowned. "Unless somebody did know and has been keeping it close to their chest? But who?"

Silvan scanned the contents of the email again. "Or maybe Derek had been working for The Mori, but at some point he had a change of heart. He kept back some of the chemicals to use as proof of what they were up to... but didn't know who to share that information with."

Gwyn pointed at me. "The obvious person to share with would be Alf. He must have known of her reputation as a witch, and he knew all about the inn of course."

"We'd even met. Albeit briefly." I took the letter back from Silvan. "Derek loved the outdoors." I thought of his allotment and all the time he had invested there, and the beautiful front garden at his cottage. Charity and Millicent had often remarked upon all the walking he did with Sunny, his Yorkie. "He must have had second thoughts." I felt sad for him. The Mori had enticed him with financial rewards, but sometimes your conscience gets the better of you. If he'd had an inkling that The Mori were planning to destroy the countryside around Whittlecombe, he wouldn't have liked that. He'd lived in the village virtually his whole life.

"When you take one step towards the darkness, you can easily be sucked in, Alf." A familiar voice made me look up.

Erik Daemonne, the ghost of my father, had

apparated into the kitchen, looking tired but otherwise well.

"Dad!"

Gwyn sniffed. "Ah Erik. You've finally made it home, have you? I've been trying to reach you for weeks."

"Well I'm here now," Erik smiled.

"Not before time!" I said. I was mightily pleased to see him of course, but it might have helped if he'd been with us a little earlier.

"I heard you might need some reinforcements. I've set up a team from the Circle of Querkus in Speckled Wood. They'll camp out there and keep an eye on things."

He rubbed his hands together, another witch who loved a good fight. "So why don't you fill me in on what's been happening?"

I made it to bed eventually and fell asleep as soon as my head hit the pillow. The clash and clatter of crockery jolted me from troubled dreams only a few hours later. Breakfast was well underway in the bar, and Charity was having to cope without me.

I sat up and flung my legs over the side of the

bed, acknowledging Mr Hoo's continuing absence. Today I had to make it a priority to get down to Millicent's cottage and see how he was doing.

Intent on grabbing a quick shower I jumped up but feeling wobbly and off-kilter I sat back down quickly. "Whoops." I clutched my head. "This is no time to get sick myself." I tried again, mooching gingerly into the bathroom and staring at my pale face in the mirror, black circles under my bloodshot eyes. "I need a holiday."

I hadn't enjoyed a holiday in years. I'd never earned enough as a bartender and then, even though I'd started managing my own bars, I'd been unable to find the time. It had to have been eight years since I'd made it on to an aeroplane.

I stood under the shower for longer than was strictly necessary just to get myself clean. The water helped to revive me. Swaying beneath the flow, I imagined where I would travel to if I had the opportunity. Japan maybe? Or Egypt? Somewhere with lots of history.

I padded barefoot back into my bedroom to dry my hair and spotted George's mobile on my bedside table. I'd brought it up here so that I could charge it. Wrapping myself in a towel I scooted quickly through to the office, ignoring the curious looks from

Penelope, Ross and the rest still hard at work analysing data, and plugged it into the charger I kept by my desk.

Then I forgot about it for a while and continued with my day.

After joining Charity to assist with the tail-end of breakfast and helping her clear up, I grabbed a quick bite myself—Monsieur Emietter makes the best scrambled eggs—before heading back to my office to hand over the papers and letters we'd taken from Piddlecombe Farm.

Penelope was pleased, or what passed for pleased in Penelope's world. She offered a tight little smile and murmured, "Wonderful" at me, before turning her attention back to her team of technical wizards. Ross kept his head down, spirit-tapping away at the keyboard and frowning in concentration.

"Oh by the way," Penelope called as I turned about, intent on taking a brisk stroll into the village to see Millicent and Mr Hoo, as I'd promised myself. "Wizard Shadowmender asked if you'd care to give him a call when you're not too busy."

I nodded. She meant now. I couldn't keep Wizard Shadowmender waiting.

I retrieved the orb from its safe place in my bedroom and perched on my window seat, holding it up to the light and watching it sparkle. "Paging Wizard Shadowmender," I said to it, rather ironically, because it worked perfectly well simply by thinking of him. The globe grew hazy, filling with billowy white clouds, pricked through with tiny spots of silvery shininess, before clearing and allowing the elderly wizard's face to emerge in front of me.

"Alf!" he called as though I were far away. "How sweet of you to contact me."

I smiled. "As if I'd pass up any opportunity."

"Penelope has been filling me in on what her team are up to, and I understand you've been risking your neck to bring her fresh data and evidence."

"Kind of." The past few days had certainly been hairy.

"Ross Baines was a wonderful find, by the way."

I couldn't help but agree. "More luck than judgement there, really."

"Nonetheless, credit where credit is due." I nodded into the orb, waiting. There had to be a reason he'd wanted me to call. A couple of beats and then, "Alf?"

Here it came.

"About your dark companion." I steeled myself. Of course he had heard all about Silvan by now, if not from Millicent or Gwyn, then certainly from Penelope. There was no way she'd withhold such information.

"I can explain—" I began.

"There's no need." The old wizard's voice was soft, his face sympathetic. "I know how desperately you've been wanting to find DS Gilchrist."

"I do." Tears pricked unexpectedly at my eyelids. I dashed them away impatiently. I had no time to get maudlin. "I didn't think I could do it on my own with my limited magickal knowledge. Silvan is a great teacher."

Wizard Shadowmender acknowledged this. "I understand the reason for the choices you've made. The only thing I would suggest is that you take great care, Alf. It may be that you do not need to tread where he does. We all of us have our own path."

"I'll remember that," I said gratefully.

He let the subject drop. "How is young Finbarr this morning?"

"He went off to the hospital in a taxi first thing.

Gwyn thinks his arm was shattered when we were attacked by our friends early this morning."

"Yes, she told me that." So Gwyn had been in touch with Wizard Shadowmender since the previous evening. My, she worked fast at times. Probably while I slept. "I'm sure they'll put him right soon enough, but I can always have one of our own see to him. If necessary I can arrange that for you."

"That would probably be a good idea," I answered, relieved that Finbarr would get the best of care.

"So what's next for you, Alf? What about Vance?" Gwyn had filled him in on our meeting with Vance too.

"I'm hoping Penelope will turn up something that will help me locate George. As soon as I have George back, then I can move on to Vance's mission and we can fix the water situation."

One step at a time. This had become my mantra. Anxiety burned away at me with every minute that passed, and I seemed no closer to achieving anything.

"You are doing well, Alf. Don't doubt it." I felt relief at being given the elderly wizard's reassurance. He continued, "I understand Erik has re-joined you today, with some of the other members of the Circle of Querkus. They've been fighting a group of The

Mori in Scotland. Given that they've finished up there for now, I'm going to send you some reinforcements. They'll be with you shortly."

At last! "Thank you, Wizard Shadowmender. They are sorely needed here."

"You need never feel alone, Alf," Wizard Shadowmender reminded me, and tipped a wink before waving and disappearing. The orb clouded over, sparkled and abruptly cleared. Just glass once more.

I wrapped it in its velvet cloth and stowed it carefully away.

If I wanted to visit the village I needed to go now, before the lunchtime service began here at the inn.

Time to skedaddle.

My first stop was Whittle Stores where Rhona was behind the counter, looking cheerier than she had been in days.

I greeted her with a hug. "How's Stan?"

Her face flooded with relief. "He's so much better, Alf. He's been struggling to keep anything down, even liquids, but they set him up on a drip and rehydrated him, and now after a few days of that he's started accepting food. His colour is better. He's definitely turned a corner."

"I'm so glad to hear that." I pondered briefly on whether it was possible to flush the forest around Whittlecombe out. Maybe a rain storm. Could we put Speckled Wood on a drip?

"Do you know, I've never mentioned this before, Alf, but when the Fayre was on across the road, I went to see this fortune teller. I can't remember what her name was—"

Fabulous Fenella. I grimaced inwardly.

"...But she foretold that Stan would end up in hospital. She even told me to keep him away from the water. I should have listened to her."

Yes, I wish you had listened to me, I thought. But even I hadn't put two and two together. Who would have imagined that what had happened to Stan would be just the start of this catastrophic chain of events? Without him going into the water how would we have been alerted to what was happening?

"How could you have possibly known what she meant?" I soothed her. "And let's not forget, Stan was trying to save the little boy. If it hadn't been Stan who fell ill after going into the water at Whittle Folly, it would have been someone else. Maybe a whole host of kids."

"Well that's true. We have to be grateful for small mercies, and it looks like he's out of the woods." Rhona changed the subject. "So how are you doing, Alf?"

"I'm fine," I lied.

"Any word on George's whereabouts?"

I shook my head. "Not yet. But we're remaining hopeful."

"Some local bobbies were down from Exeter asking questions the other day."

"At least they're still taking his disappearance seriously," I said. They hadn't sought me out though.

I collected together a few bits and bobs to take round to Millicent—two packets of biscuits and a pint of milk. A couple of women entered the shop, took a surreptitious glance at me and sniffed in disapproval.

"And what about the villagers?" Rhona asked loudly as she ran through the items. "Are they being a little kinder to you?"

I shot a look at the other two customers. They seemed suddenly fascinated by the boxed cereals. "About the supposed source of the poisonous water being in Speckled Wood, you mean?" I glowered at the window, watching one or two people walking by, averting their eyes as they spotted me inside. That had been the story of the past week, people grumbling whenever I was in their vicinity, or glaring at me. Fortunately nobody had been physically aggressive, just passively hostile.

"It's complete batpoop, but I'll live with it." I sighed. My twelve months at Whittle Inn had seen my reputation plummet to new depths and soar to great heights. It was a rollercoaster for sure.

"You're a stronger woman than I am, Alf."

I doubted that. Here she was keeping body and soul together and still running her business while her husband lay in intensive care. "Give my love to Stan, Rhona," I smiled and left, holding my head up.

Mr Hoo blinked at me sleepily from the nest of cushions Millicent had created in her living room. I stroked his feathery head and his little sticky-up ears. "Hello, my darling friend," I said. "How are you?"

"I fancy he's a little better, but I still can't entice him to eat anything," Millicent said from behind me.

"I just spoke to Rhona in the shop," I said, without turning around. "She says Stan is improving. He's started to tolerate fluids. He's been on a drip to rehydrate him."

Millicent came to stand next to me. "I've never tried a drip on an owl, I have to be honest."

I put my arm around her shoulders and squeezed her. She looked as weary as I felt. "I know you're doing your best," I said. "I wasn't criticising."

"I hate that there are hundreds, maybe thousands of animals in the woods that I can't help."

I nodded solemnly. Jasper whimpered. I reached out to him and he ambled forwards to stick his head between my knees.

"I've been giving all my animals bottled water. Mary Brigstone's dog got sick after walking in the woods."

"They should close off access," I exclaimed in horror. "Nobody should be exercising their animals anywhere near standing water. Surely the Water Board have told them that?"

"Well have you not noticed?" Millicent asked in surprise. "When was the last time you saw a member of the Water Board in Whittlecombe?"

I stared at Millicent in shock. She was right. The tanks of water were being replenished on a daily basis, but other than that, I hadn't seen the familiar livery of the water company's vans for several days. Perhaps not since the village meeting.

They had sown the seeds of doubt and despair,

vilified the name of Whittle Inn, and then done a runner.

"By all that's sacred," I growled. "How dare they? They dug an enormous hole in my beer cellar and they haven't filled it in yet!"

CHAPTER SEVENTEEN

"I have made you a potion, *mein Honigbär*."

Frau Krause peered up at me from below her grey fringe, her piercing blue eyes glinting in the soft evening light. We were wrapping up dinner service and I had started clearing her plates away.

"That's kind of you," I smiled, eyeing the tiny vial of green coloured sludge she was holding out in my direction.

"*Die schlafhilfe*." She tucked her hands against her cheek and mimed falling asleep.

"A sleeping potion?" I suppose I did look tired. I intended to get to bed sharpish this evening.

Frau Krause nodded enthusiastically. "I like to use the leaves and barks and sap of trees that sleep in the winter. They know how to take a nap." She laughed merrily and I took the potion from her. Frau Krause was a regular guest at Whittle Inn and enjoyed spending a great deal of her free time in the forest surrounding us.

"You didn't use the water from the forest did you?" I had of course warned her about the situation with the poison in the water sources.

"Just a little."

I held the small test-tube shaped bottle up to the window and looked at it. Frau Krause obviously didn't believe in filtering to make her potions clear. You could definitely make out some sediment. I shuddered inwardly.

"Don't be concerned," Frau Krause said, reaching out to pat the hand that held the potion. "I made this one at home in Deutschland. It is not from here. It is good stuff. It helps you sleep. I use it all the time." She cackled loudly, ensuring everyone in the vicinity looked around at us, then excused herself, heading upstairs to her room. No doubt she'd be back out in the woods within the hour.

I slipped the vial into my pocket and resumed clearing her table, lost in thought about Frau Krause's potion abilities, until I heard a commotion originating from the kitchen. I recognised Monsieur Emietter's voice from the loud French curses and heard the sound of pots and pans flying and crashing around.

Several of the guests, who were still seated at tables and finishing their meals, tittered.

I put on my best reassuring smile and headed for the frosted glass door that separated the bar and the back passage to the kitchen. As I reached it half a dozen of Finbarr's pixies streamed past me clutching chunks of cake and chicken legs. Obviously they'd decided, in Finbarr's absence, that they were hungry and had robbed the kitchen.

Unfortunately, Charity picked that moment to walk out from behind the bar with a tray full of drinks, including several glasses of red wine. One of the pixies collided with Charity's knees, and jolted her backwards, the tray of drinks collapsed into her chest.

"What the—?" she screeched. "You little—! I'm going to—"

I rapidly uttered a muting spell to drown out a train of expletives. I watched the pixies disappear out of the front door then turned to help Charity clear up.

"Look at the state of me!" Red wine had soaked through her white shirt.

I dabbed at her with some paper towels. My attempts to clean up were ineffective of course. "You need to get that straight in the wash."

247

Charity groaned. "What a nuisance. I only put a load in a few hours ago."

We tried to conserve energy and water where possible at Whittle Inn, and Charity was especially energy-conscious, particularly now the water was severely rationed. "That's always the way." I laughed.

"Do you have anything you want to throw in? Kill two birds with one stone?"

I thought of the robes I'd been wearing while visiting Piddlecombe Farm the night before, walking through the mud of the farmyard, the cow pats, and then exploring that stinking house. They certainly needed a wash. "As it happens, I do," I replied. "Leave your shirt in the machine and I'll throw my bits in later."

Charity disappeared to get changed and I finished clearing up after the dinner service with the help of Florence. I then spent some time appeasing Monsieur Emietter, although given Gwyn's absence I had no translator so he couldn't understand what I was attempting to say. It took me a while to calm him down and restore order to the kitchen. Finally, I was able to clump up the back stairs to my suite of rooms and pop my head into the office.

Penelope Quigwell had some staying power, I'll give her that. She was wrapped in conversation with someone on the phone. Ross looked up briefly, caught my eye and waved. I'd never seen him looking happier.

Rather than interrupt, I grabbed George's phone from where it had been sitting charging all day and beat a hasty retreat to my bedroom. The clothes I'd peeled off before hitting the sack this morning, lay in a crumpled pile at the foot of my bed. I switched George's phone on, to make sure it had charged, and set it down beside me on the bed while it binged and chimed as messages and emails flooded through, one after another.

They seemed to go on for the longest time.

I picked up the phone and flicked past the home screen. It hadn't been password protected. That surprised me. George was a copper after all.

I noted lots of work emails and messages from concerned colleagues. It would be good to return George to the people who loved him, I thought with a twang.

I wondered whether he had any photos of me stored on his phone, or of us together, and so I flipped through the photo album while the rest of the messages continued to come in.

What I saw there gave me pause.

My heart sank.

George with another woman. Looking cosy.

The photos had been taken at—or around—the time of the Fayre. He had the fake tattoos and the shaved head. The pair of them were cheek to cheek in a few of the shots—big broad smiles. She was kissing his cheek in another, her arm clamped firmly around his neck.

I stared at the photos until my vision blurred. It could be entirely innocent, I told myself. So why did I feel so hurt?

I threw the phone on the bed, my stomach a hard rock of despair, staring into space for what seemed an eon until it beeped again, releasing me from the paralysis of my mood of despondency.

"I do not have time for this," I hissed fiercely. "One thing at a time."

I gathered myself together, ignoring the phone, and finally I remembered the laundry.

I considered calling Florence to take the clothes back down to the utility area next to the kitchen for me so that I could just hit the sack, but that did seem the height of indolence given that I'd told Charity I would do the washing. Besides Florence was still tidying up after our guests.

I picked up my pile of clothes and carried them back downstairs, tossing everything piece by piece into the machine. I paused when I reached my robes, fishing the sleeves out the right way, and patting down the pockets. I could feel something in one of them.

I rummaged around and located the small square jewellery box I'd extracted from the woman's jacket found hanging over the chair in the room in the cellar. I'd forgotten all about it.

I flipped the lid to expose the contents, expecting a bracelet or a chunky ring, and did a double take.

A prism-shaped jewel nestled inside. Gloriously red, like a London bus or a post box, but shining brighter than the moon on a clear night. I fumbled with it, my fingers suddenly feeling incredibly fat and clumsy, and lifted it out of the box. It couldn't have been more than an inch-and-a-half tall, and less than half that wide, and yet the light it threw out filled the utility room with a rich, warm glow. I held it up to the light, staring into the centre of it. Was it my imagination or could I see tiny gold sparkles at the core?

"What are you?" I asked in wonder. "And why

were you left behind at that farm house?" I twisted it this way and that, examining it from different angles. "I suppose you could be something innocuous like a ruby or maybe a semi-precious stone," I said. In itself it didn't appear to be dangerous. It could just be a coincidence that it was in a jacket, in a house known to have been occupied by The Mori.

"I ought to show you to somebody," I told it, and then yawned. "But maybe I'll do that in the morning."

Frau Krause's potion did the trick, and I slept like a baby, although I probably wouldn't have required much rocking in any case if the truth be known. My mother had always said that an hour before midnight was worth two after and so when I awoke at some-time before three, I already felt deeply rested.

I lay blinking in the darkness, wondering what had woken me and whether I'd be able to drift back to sleep. I turned on my side with the intention of doing just that and let my eyes flicker shut once more.

But something wasn't right.

I couldn't tell what. I lay there, pretending to

sleep, but eventually, my sense of unease won. I pushed myself into a sitting position, wishing Mr Hoo was here, and reached out with my senses.

Whittle Inn was quiet, apart from the sounds I might have expected – hushed creaks and groans as the old building cooled overnight. If I paid attention I could hear the snores of sleeping guests. From downstairs at the rear of the inn came the gentle roar of the boiler, topping its own hot water up, ready for all the guests who would require baths and showers in the morning.

My window was open, but I could neither hear nor sense the movement of small nocturnal animals or birds. There was neither the ribbiting of a toad nor the chirruping of a grasshopper. And not a breath of wind.

The world was holding its breath.

I didn't like it.

I untangled myself from my bedclothes and grabbed a scrunchie from my bedside table, tying my hair back. Then I reached for my wand.

I padded to the open window and peered out into the darkness. At first glance everything seemed normal. Nothing to see. But as my eyes adjusted to the different light level out there, I spotted movement in a distant hedge. A red glow.

Further away, Speckled Wood was covered by a glowing green aura. The Circle of Querkus were on guard there, and by the looks of it they were alarmed.

"Gwyn," I called into the darkness, as quietly and urgently as I could. Despite her many faults, and her haughty stand-offishness on occasions, I understood instinctively that I could rely on my great grandmother in a crisis. I knew she would be alerted by my tone. She appeared next to me almost instantly. I pointed with my wand out of the window in the direction of the red globe. She saw it, not much more than a pinprick of light. She understood immediately.

"Rouse everyone," I told her, my voice low. "Tell them to gather in the bar. Move swiftly and quietly."

She nodded and vanished, and I heard a creak from the floorboards somewhere above me. Gwyn had elected to wake Silvan first.

The chances were that Penelope Quigwell and her wizards were still awake and working. On bare feet I padded softly to my door and pulled it gently open, inch by inch. With the coast clear I crept onto the landing and turned for my office door. I hadn't made it halfway when I heard a buzz.

I swung about while simultaneously dropping to a crouch, sending out a vicious ball of fire in the direction of the sound. My aim was true. A red orb exploded, scattering baking hot fragments along the corridor.

"Silvan!" I screeched. The game was up, no need for stealth anymore. Footsteps thundered along the landing above rapidly followed by another explosion. The door next to me opened and something shot a hot ray of burning energy above my head. I heard Penelope shriek and stumble backwards. Silvan crashed down the stairs to the side of me, rolling into a crouch, his wand poised and pointing at the space behind me. I turned my head as he took aim, and another red orb smashed to the floor.

"Penelope? Are you alright?" I called.

"Absolutely fine," she returned, sounding remarkably like her usual cool and poised self.

I crawled towards the door until I could peer in. Ross—like all the ghosts—had disappeared leaving just Penelope and her two technology wizards alone. I figured neither of them had seen much in the way of combat, and I couldn't be sure about Penelope either. "We need to get down to the bar area and group together," I told her.

"We're right behind you," she said.

I heard other doors opening on the floor above me. That would be the guests coming out of their rooms. I cast a quick glance at Silvan. "Charity," I said with a grimace. The inn was currently half-full and comprised witches, ghosts, and several sages. For the most part they could take care of themselves, perhaps even help us out if the need arose, but Charity, despite what Gwyn and Millicent said, was virtually powerless.

"Don't worry," Silvan said. "Gwyn and Florence are going to escort her down here."

Florence? What could Florence do? Bash The Mori over the head with her feather duster?

But I had no time for anything else. "To the bar everyone!" I yelled up the stairs, and then Silvan and I made a run for it.

Shafts of heat were shot at me from all directions as I tumbled down the final flight of stairs and pounded along the downstairs passage. We burst through into the bar and I waved my wand to illuminate the room. The lights came on as Penelope and her partners scampered in after us, several guests hot on their heels. From the main staircase came the sharp sounds of more explosions and Charity crying out. I wanted to go and help her, but Silvan grabbed the neck of my nightshirt and yanked me back.

"Do you hear that?" he asked, and we all became

still, listening to the sound of numerous angry hornets.

Not just one member of The Mori. Not even half a dozen. Perhaps not even the group we'd encountered during the Battle for Speckled Wood.

Judging by the volume and the chorus of buzzing there were a battalion of them, and they had managed to infiltrate the inn.

Silvan, Penelope and I stood back to back, the other witches and wizards—many clad in their nightwear—joining us. Frau Krause, dressed in a long and frilly Victorian style bedgown, her wand drawn, her lips pulled back in a fearless sneer, appeared especially fierce.

"How did they get in?" I asked in confusion. "How did they break through Mr Kephisto's magickal barrier?" But even as I uttered the words, I watched as a spinning red globe drifted past the window, seeming to rise out of the ground and all at once I understood.

"Oh no. No no no."

They were rising out of the ground. The beer cellar to be exact. They were using the external entrance. I'd been the fool who'd let Norbert from the water board dig down into the well, and no doubt this was exactly what The Mori had planned all along. I'd fallen for their ploy hook, line and sinker.

Charity and the last few guests scuttled down the front stairs into the bar. I grabbed her arm. "Stand next to me," I said, "and don't do anything brave or reckless."

"As if I would," she muttered.

At that moment all the lights in the inn were extinguished. A few people gasped.

"On guard," instructed Silvan, lighting his wand and casting shadows around the room. I bent at the knees, taking up a defence stance.

"Alf?" said a voice I recognised intimately. A voice I'd yearned for. "Alf? Don't shoot at them. It's me. If you shoot at them they say they're going to kill me."

George.

CHAPTER EIGHTEEN

"Don't shoot at them Alf. They've told me to tell you that you're surrounded. There are hundreds of them here. Under the building. Hiding in the hedges, waiting to break down the barrier. If you don't surrender instantly, they're going to kill everyone, starting with me."

"We'll never surrender!" growled Silvan with fury.

"George?" I called, and Silvan lit the room with his wand. There by the main door to the bar stood my beau, looking thinner than when I'd seen him last, pale and a little unkempt, in need of a shave and a hair wash, but nonetheless, it was him.

Despite myself, in spite of the photos, my heart tripped over itself with happiness at seeing him again. But I wished with all my heart it had not been under these circumstances, with dozens and do of The Mori intent on destroying my inn and possibly terminating me.

"Lay down your wands," George repeated the words he'd been told to say. I met his eyes. They sparkled with rebellion. I was relieved to see that he too was prepared to fight alongside me.

"Hundreds?" I asked him.

He nodded.

"No surrender," Silvan repeated doggedly.

I lay a placating hand on my dark instructor's arm. "A wand is merely a tool," I reminded him. Hadn't I been practising my own brand of magick my whole life long, until very recently, with little more than the palm of my hand or a pointed finger?

I met his black eyes, so deep and dark, but far from soulless. Here was a man who would fight to the death for a cause he believed in. The corner of his mouth twitched, and he dropped his wand hand. Together we lay our wands on the ground. The other witches in the room followed suit.

The door of the inn burst open and eight or nine gl᠎ᵉˢplendent in red and gold sparkles, floated᠎ ᠎om. They quickly surrounded us. One of᠎ ᠎George and he cried out in pain.

᠎ ᠎d angrily and Silvan lifted his hand

to direct a burst of energy at the globe. It spun on him and sparks flew.

"No!" I shouted and pushed Silvan out of the way. Too late. He fell to his knees clutching his chest. He raised his hands once more, to dispense swift justice. I knocked against him, spoiling his aim, then stood defiantly in front of him, determined he would not be hurt.

"Alfhild." From the drive outside I heard someone calling my name. The disembodied voice sent chills running through my spine. I recognised that voice. The man who had abducted me the day before George went missing.

Casting a worried glance at Silvan, hoping he would remain calm and not provoke The Mori into further retaliation, I walked slowly to the door. I followed a deep thrumming sound, side-stepping the globes that spun and rotated around me, watching my every move, supervising me every step of the way.

An enormous globe spun above the lawn, reminding me of the one I'd last seen Jed inhabiting in Speckled Wood. The size of a small family car, it slowed to a stop as I edged towards it, then dissipated in a bubbling explosion of gold glitter. A tall man stepped forwards to confront me.

"Hello again, Alfhild," he said, and my vision greyed slightly at the edges as I recalled the night this man had almost drowned me.

Fury sparked within me. How dare he treat my friends like this? I took rapid steps towards him intent on a showdown. Instantly, two globes the size of beach balls closed in on me, buzzing their angry hornet noise. I halted and glared at him with intense hatred instead.

"Ah you remember me." He laughed, the sound lightly floating on the night air.

"I remember you," I retorted. "But I don't know who you are." If I could have shot bolts of lightning out of my eyes I would have done.

He shrugged, so cavalier. "My name is James Edward Bailey. I believe you knew my son."

Jed!

"Knew him and banished him from my land." I straightened my back. "Just like I'm going to do for you."

This time his laugh was a roar of genuine humour and I bristled in response.

"Oh, Alfhild." His voice wheedled away at my indignation. "How sweet. Do you really have no concept of who I am or how powerful we are?"

"You're the leader of The Mori?" I asked, making

a brave attempt to sound unafraid, but I have to be honest, of course I felt shaken to the core. I hoped nobody else could hear the tremble in my voice. Where was my father? Now would be a really good time for the cavalry to arrive.

"Me? Goodness no. Not me. I'm just a General in these parts. A cog in a magnificent machine. And you—my dear—have been jamming up our gears. We're getting a bit fed up with you."

"You were the one who tried to drown me in the village pond?"

He smiled, his eyes icy. "Yes. You'll have to tell me how you managed to extricate yourself from that situation. I thought we'd achieved our aim that night."

"Friends in watery places." I looked around at the other spinning globes. Who were they all? "You weren't alone that night."

"Well I too have friends, Alfhild."

I sneered at the idea. "I somehow doubt that."

The pretence of the smile plastered on James's face fell away. "Anyhow this is tiresome. I have plenty of business to get through tonight."

I looked in confusion at Speckled Wood. Where was Erik? And the Circle of Querkus? Why weren't they here fighting back against these reprehensible bullies?

James followed my glance. "There will be no-one rushing to your aid tonight, Alfhild. Your father and his cronies have been rounded up in the wood, and we've cast our own forcefield to hold them secure until we have no further need of them."

Need of them? That sounded ominous. What did he mean?

"You have consistently underestimated the power of dark magick, seeming to prefer the notion that your magick—good magick—can right all wrongs and solve all problems. Well, tonight I'll finally have the chance to school you in a few home truths."

James walked the few steps towards me and drew his wand—long, thin and black, it looked like a skeleton's charred and crooked finger. He tapped me on the chin, and I experienced a sharp pain which briefly flared and then died back. "Your Wizard Shadowmender seems to have deserted you in your hour of need, doesn't he? Poor Alfhild."

I lifted my fingers to my chin and glanced down at them. Blood pooled between my index and middle finger.

"What are you going to do to me?" I asked, lifting my gaze to his.

264

"What am I going to do? I'm going to kill all your friends, banish your ghosts and burn the inn to the ground. That's what I'm going to do for starters." I stared at him in revulsion. "Then I'll have you torn limb from limb, but only after you've begged me to do so."

He threw his head back and laughed loudly. "It's going to be so much fun, Alfhild."

"I'll never beg for you," I spat.

"Oh I think you will." He composed himself and moved closer to me, tapping my left shoulder lightly with his wand. Yet again I felt the sharp pain, this time more deeply in the tissue. I cried out and jabbed my hand to where he'd hurt me. More blood flowed between my fingertips.

"But first, before we attend to the interesting part of the evening, I believe you have something of mine."

What did he mean? "Do I?" I asked, puzzled. "Not that I'm aware of."

He lifted his wand again and I cringed. "I'm a patient man generally, but I do have a lot to do. Just tell me where to find it, Alfhild."

I shook my head. "Find what? What do I have?"

"A Moridot."

I frowned in confusion. "A Moridot?"

"The cornerstone of The Mori's power is the Morimonolitus. A Moridot is a stone cut from the Morimonolitus. I believe you may have stumbled across it when you trespassed on my farm the other night."

The red stone I'd found? That's what it was? If that was the case then I'd unearthed a treasure indeed. There was no way on our good green earth that I was handing something that precious back to James.

"I don't know what you mean." I dissembled, trying to think on my feet. "I went to Piddlecombe Farm in search of my fiancé. We didn't take anything from there."

"You're a terrible liar, Alfhild," growled James, lifting his wand again, impatient to get down to the business of causing me more pain.

I know I am. I dropped my head, studying the blood on my fingers, whilst avoiding his intense scrutiny. I moved my feet apart, relaxed into attack stance, my knees loosely flexed beneath my nightshirt, my shoulders rolled back.

"We'll take the inn apart brick by brick, beam by beam if we have to. We will find it. With or without your help."

I remained silent. If what I had in the little jewel

box meant that much to him, then perhaps my inn seemed a fair exchange.

"And of course we can start by eliminating a few of your friends."

He gestured at a globe spinning alongside him. "Go in there and pick someone. Anyone." It buzzed happily off. "In fact, make it the boyfriend," James called after it. "Drag him out here."

George.

James would kill him.

I had to act.

Now.

If ever there was a time to remember everything Silvan had taught me, this was it.

I felt the dirt beneath my bare feet, grounded myself on the earth of Whittle Estate, and drew strength from the Daemonnes who had come before me. I envisioned the women of Whittlecombe who had lost their lives at the hands of men driven by hatred, much like The Mori.

And I drew on the fear and anxiety I'd experienced after losing my father, and the discontent at the relationship I'd had with my mother. I recalled the anger and hurt that had followed in the wake of Jed's betrayal, and the fear and loathing The Mori had instilled in me every time they came after me.

I pooled all of that with my anger at the pain and suffering this rotten organisation had caused Finbarr and Silvan, and Stan and Godfrey, and Mr Hoo. And not forgetting poor Derek Pearce who had lost his life simply because he'd tried to take a stand against his oppressors.

I garnered all those negative emotions, sucked them up from deep within me, up into my stomach, then my chest and into my shoulders, down into my arms and to my fingertips.

Then, with my head tucked down I poked at my chin, pressing the edges of the injury together to harvest fresh drops of my own blood. With them sticky on my fingers, I spoke my spell loudly and clearly.

A witch's curse using a witch's blood, is not one to be cast lightly.

Sinking through my hips, I threw my head back and fixed James in my gaze, flinging my right hand forward and spraying him with the drops of blood I'd gathered, sending every ounce of magickal power I had his way. *"Corrupta es qui es, crescas in fletu influunt et infirma!"*

And what a spell I cast.

The force of it knocked me backwards.

Several things happened at once. He tried to block my attack and failed, only deflecting it in part, by twisting sideways. He screamed, and with a kick of his wand hand sent a ball of malicious energy my way. Already off balance I continued to drop, just as Silvan had drilled into me, time and time again.

I hit the ground, rolled, then bounced back onto my feet, squatting in a crouch, sending pulses of energy at the globes that spun around us, knocking them about. They spun in confusion like billiard balls on a slippery surface.

I'd done some damage to James even if I hadn't wiped him out completely. His left arm hung uselessly by his side and as he hopped towards me, he had the appearance of a man who'd suffered a sudden stroke. I sent another bolt of energy his way for good measure and made a dash towards the inn.

George was coming out, the spinning globe James had sent inside buzzed angrily at head height, pushing George ahead of itself. As I lifted my hand to cast a new spell at George's captor, I heard James shout from behind me. "Kill them! Kill them all!"

Before the globe could do anything else, I sent a

deadly curse its way. It shattered into a million burning pieces with a spine-shuddering squeal.

"George, get down," I yelled as he looked around in consternation. He dropped to all fours and rolled back towards the protection of the external wall of the inn, throwing his hands over his head to protect himself. He glanced up at me as I took out another couple of globes, but everywhere I looked there appeared to be more and more of them. I couldn't fight an army on my own.

"Silvan," I cried, hoping he could hear me and wasn't badly injured. "I need you!"

A flash of light from the ground blinded me, and a pain shot through my ankle. James had resumed firing at me. I hopped onto one foot in agony and he shot at my good leg. I fell to the ground and he was on me, his wand pointed at my neck, the tip digging into my jugular.

"I'll cut your head off," he snarled and in that instant I knew I was done for. I'd failed. Everything would be for nothing. George would be killed, and Charity and Silvan, and everyone else I loved along with him.

James would banish my ghosts. My beloved wonky inn would burn, and Speckled Wood and all its inhabitants would be allowed to die.

Think only of love, I told myself, and breathed in, the faces of all those who meant something to me forming in my mind's eye.

"No!" A voice, oddly familiar and unexpected, erupted from the darkness out of nowhere.

A bolt of bright red lightning blasted through the sky above me, and the pressure on my neck eased as James crumpled to the ground. I pushed myself to sitting, and observed James sprawled beside me, evidently dead, his eyes staring glassily in my direction. Silvan burst through the door behind me, his wand raised, blasting away at globes as they spun around us. "Alf?" he called.

But I focused instead, on the figure who had come to my rescue, and my jaw dropped. Tall, over six-feet, muscular build. Looking rougher than the last time I'd seen him, stubble on his cheeks, wrinkles around tired cornflower blue eyes.

"Jed?" I whispered.

He cast an inscrutable look my way. "The very same," he nodded and winked, then swivelled about to face Speckled Wood, and lifted his hands. "*Et claustra cadunt*," he ordered. *Let the barriers fall.*

And they did.

The battle that followed was vicious, but ultimately fairly short-lived.

I dragged myself back to where George was sheltering. We held each other as a firestorm erupted around our heads. The Circle of Querkus—in their spinning green globe forms—broke out of the woods as the barrier fell. They set upon The Mori with deadly and unforgiving intent. It was no surprise at all to see them joined by Wizard Shadowmender and Mr Kephisto. Neither of the elderly wizards were ever far away when I desperately needed them.

They were backed up by a gleeful Silvan, who led a posse of the current Whittle Inn guests in a flanking action. I watched in bemusement as Frau Krauss and Gwyn worked together, rounding up several of the spinning globes and incapacitating them, each exhibiting a light and lethally-accurate touch with their wands.

Jed stood among it all, seemingly unsure what to do or what his role should be—perhaps unclear which side he truly belonged with. The Mori, without a leader were directionless. They fell back to the boundaries of Whittle Inn and rapidly dispersed under relentless fire from Erik and his friends.

In less than ten minutes an ecstatic cheer

erupted around the grounds and Silvan ran back to me in jubilation.

"We've seen them off," he reported. "Are you alright?"

"I'll live," I replied. "It's only my ankle."

George stood and pulled me gently to my feet. "You're bleeding," he said.

"It's nothing. Surface wounds." But I already knew that one of the first things I'd be doing would be to ask Millicent to create a deep cleansing potion to rid me of any corruption James had thought to poison me with, no doubt stored within the core of his wand.

"So this is the famous George?" Silvan asked, scrutinizing my fiancé with curiosity.

"Yes." I nodded over his shoulder. "And this is Jed."

George and Jed regarded each other suspiciously, while Silvan looked them both up and down in amusement. "My, my," he said, eyes sparkling with fresh amusement. "What a tangled web."

I glared at him, as Erik ran up to us, his wand aimed at Jed.

Jed held his hands up in surrender.

"Dad," I said. "Jed was the one to finish off James. And drop the barrier."

"He's The Mori," my father reminded me as though I'd forgotten, his face stern. "He can't be allowed to go free."

I looked at Jed, and then at Erik. "Look, just give us a minute, can you?"

My father nodded, reluctantly and stepped back. All of about two paces.

"Dad!"

"Alright, alright," he said and retreated another few steps.

I tutted and indicated to Jed we would walk in the opposite direction. George followed me.

"Two minutes, okay?" I repeated and looking slightly hurt he joined my father.

I reached for Jed and linked my arm through his, partly because I needed the support in order to be able to walk steadily, but also because mixed emotions were jumbling my thoughts and I wasn't entirely sure what I should be thinking or feeling.

"How did you manage to come back?" I asked. "I thought I'd banished you."

Jed grimaced. "Your magick is no match for the combined power of The Mori." He said this without sounding boastful, simply highlighted it as a fact.

"And are you still The Mori?" I asked.

He studied the corpse of his father lying on the

lawn in front of us, his face strangely neutral. "I don't know who or what I am now," he answered. "I have a feeling the Circle of Querkus will get to decide that in the future."

"What do *you* want though?"

"I think that's kind of a moot point, Alf. I'll probably never have my freedom again."

His face turned bleak in the subdued light as we considered his future. The lines around his eyes spoke of the strain he'd been living under for the past twelve months.

Wizard Shadowmender had appeared in our peripheral vision. I nodded at him, and Jed and I stopped walking. The time had come for me to hand Jed over to those who had a purpose for him.

"Thank you for what you did today," I said softly. "I wouldn't have made it without you." I wished I could help him. He had saved my life after all, and those of my friends.

He shrugged, tired and careworn. "I've been watching you these last few months. I would have given anything to have spoken with you once more." I thought of the spinning globe I'd seen on the night of the vampire wedding. Perhaps that had been him.

"What happened... Before," he continued, and his voice broke. "What I did. It was wrong. I regretted it right away. They gave me a mission. I couldn't dare fail them. I feared them. I was weak." He took my hands in both of his large ones and squeezed them together. "You're so strong, Alf. I'm so proud of who you've become."

I smiled, my eyes filling with tears. This man had meant so much to me and betrayed me so badly. But still, I wanted to forgive him.

"If there was anything I could do, to go some way to repair all the hurt I've caused and the damage I've done. You know I would do it."

I stared into his eyes, saw the honesty there, and the despair.

A sudden vision of Vance gave me pause. What if…?

"Well, with my father's permission, and a little help from a few of my friends, there is something you can do for us," I replied, and smiled.

CHAPTER NINETEEN

I'd hidden the Moridot among my underwear in the washing machine. After I'd added my clothes and Charity's to the wash, and thrown in a washing pod, I'd elected not to put the wash on, but to hide the jewel in there, amongst the load, until morning when I could figure out what it was and what I was supposed to do with it. It probably hadn't been the most secure place to hide a precious object, but I had been willing to wager it wouldn't be the first place anyone would look for it either.

So now I hooked it out of its hiding place and slipped it into my pocket.

Dawn was breaking as fifteen of us, and an owl carried by Millicent, paraded single file into Speckled Wood. Gwyn led the way, her wand raised, intoning—from what I could make out—some ancient spell for the wellbeing of forests.

Gwyn, Millicent and I had been joined by Wizard Shadowmender, Mr Kephisto, Silvan, Charity, Penelope Quigwell and her two technical wizards, my father Erik, Frau Krause and Finbarr. For the first time I was able to command a full Speckled Wood coven, although in reality I think Gwyn took the lead, rather than me. In addition to the thirteen witches—and bearing in mind Charity could hardly even count herself as a novice—we had brought along George and Jed.

We followed the trail deep into the wood, winding along the path between the trees. The wood had never been so quiet. Hardly a rustle among the leaves or a tweet from the bushes disturbed the early morning, at a time when the dawn chorus should have deafened us in its unrestrained joyfulness.

I had never felt the passing of time so keenly as I did on that short hike. The trees, gnarled and ancient, bent over us, their impending doom seeming certain. A forest without fresh water cannot live. I trailed my hand lightly on each trunk I passed, as I walked by these wonderful guardians of the ages, offering reassurance.

All will be well, I told them.

I hobbled slightly, my ankle tightly bound up with both a bandage from the first aid kit behind the bar and with a healing spell uttered by Millicent, but as long as I didn't intend to sprint for some imaginary finishing line somewhere, I could cope with the walk. Occasionally George reached out to help me, but I shook him off.

I could make my own way.

We shuffled quietly into the clearing in the wood. The one that surrounded Vance's pool. In the faint light of morning the water appeared more revolting than ever. Several inches of yellow and green foam floated on the surface, like the mould on a tin of beans that's been open too long.

Gwyn directed everyone to stand in a circle around the pool of water, with the exception of Jed and George who remained with me.

She floated around the circle, issuing instructions and offering words of encouragement, while I flicked off the sandals I'd chosen to wear to walk through the woods. When she came to me at the end, I murmured at her from the side of my mouth.

"Grandmama? You don't want me to do it naked this time, do you?"

She deigned to look shocked. "Certainly not, Alfhild. Whatever are you thinking?" Before I could respond she wagged her wand at me. "Now are you ready?"

"As ready as I'll ever be," I replied, and she turned to face the toxic water.

I reached inside my robes for my wand, stroking the ridges of the ancient wood, a piece of Vance I could cherish forever.

"Greetings, Vance, Keeper of the Marsh," Gwyn intoned, and the other witches in the circle repeated her in a chorus.

"Hear us as the dawn breaks, our ancient and wise friend."

"Hear us," we repeated.

"Yet again we come to you with tidings and best wishes. We bring offerings and ask that you accept these and rise to hear our plea. In the name of Nerthus, and The Nix, of Belisama and Nymue, I call you from the depths of your slumber and ask that you grant us an audience once more. Hear us Vance, we beg, as you have heard us before."

The ground around us began to vibrate and I watched enthralled as the water first rippled, the layers of foam bobbing up and down, and then began to bubble. Gently at first, then more rapidly as though the heat had been turned up beneath a cauldron. The water whipped up a fierce storm, displacing the foam to the edges of the pool where it clung to the banks and the rocks.

At last, the tips of Vance's branches, coiled like a corkscrew, broke the surface and he exploded into the air. His branches whipped around our heads as he untwisted. Water, slime and pondweed rapidly drenched all of us.

George shot backwards. "What—"

I looked back at him and shook my head slightly. He took a few reluctant steps towards me. "What is that?"

"This is Vance," I told him. "Only he can cleanse the water in Speckled Wood. We've come to seek his assistance."

"Alfhild," Vance bellowed in his deep voice. "You have returned at last."

He twitched and stretched and rolled his trunk, bending down to me, his heavy eyes scrutinizing me carefully.

"You have what I asked for?"

"I do." I gingerly stepped down into the water, good foot first, then following it up with the injured one. I limped a few feet into the water, the sludge squeezing unpleasantly between my toes.

"Alf?" George asked, stepping to the edge and reaching for me. "I don't think you should be in there."

Jed merely stood alongside Gwyn, watching me as I reached into my pockets.

I drew out my wand and the Moridot. Jed's eyes grew round, and for the first time I sensed fear.

I lay the Moridot on my palm and held it out so that Vance could see it.

"I struggled to find all that you asked," I said, "but I think I have it all now."

I turned back to Jed and George. "Guys," I said, "you should join me."

A brave heart and a bruised heart
 A true heart and a pure heart
 A dark heart and a false heart
 A pulse that beats hot and red
 And a sacrifice of the living ... and the dead.

Those were the things Vance had requested I bring him, and then and only then could he contrive to purify the water.

I had puzzled long and hard about what such things constituted since the night he had told me of his requirements. And even once I had them all in place, I had no idea what would happen when I presented them to him.

So here we all were.

Jed eased into the water readily enough, casting a nervous glance at Erik and Wizard Shadowmender as he did so. Perhaps it crossed his mind to run, perhaps it did not. George for his part was more reluctant, but I smiled at him. "It will all be okay," I said, and at last he climbed onto the rocks, close to where I stood.

I looked up at Vance. "I wasn't entirely sure whether I was looking for one person or many. In the end I think I can probably offer you everything you need between the three of us."

"Tell me," Vance commanded, his voice low and somehow terrible.

I took a deep breath. "I believe that all of us who encircle you now, have a heart that is brave. We have all fought for what we believe in. Just tonight we have rallied against the enemy once more, and beaten them away from the doors of Whittle Inn. Jed here, killed his father, to help us do so."

I swallowed. "And who among us can deny our bruised hearts? Certainly not I, dear Vance." I flicked a look at George. "I thought our love was true, but I found photos of George on his phone, with another woman."

George blanched. "On my phone? Wait. Alf, I can explain that. That's Stacey—"

"I'm sure you can," I said gently. "And one day I'd like to hear that explanation."

"It's—" George said hurriedly.

"But not now," I said and lifted my wand. "*Adipem bufo.*" With a silvery flash of light, George disappeared, to be replaced by a fat toad.

Someone behind me guffawed. Silvan.

George, the toad, croaked in confusion.

I turned my attention back to Vance. "I do believe George's heart was largely true. Love is a fickle emotion that confuses us. It is multi-faceted. Perhaps all of us experience loving many people at one time. Perhaps we shouldn't apportion guilt and blame. All I know is I need some space."

"I also bring you my owl." I reached out with my wand hand as Millicent came forward. Mr Hoo hopped onto my forearm and I held him up to the giant tree above me, before settling him on my shoulder.

"This is my most precious friend, but I offer him to you as proof of a true and pure heart."

Vance twitched and rolled, his branches raining debris down on us. I couldn't tell whether this was a good sign or not.

I held up the Moridot in my left hand. I knew how Vance loved his precious stones. "This is a Moridot. It is a piece of the Morimonolitus, a giant stone at the heart of The Mori's power." It twinkled in my hand, casting off an impressive amount of red light on our surroundings. I watched as Vance's eyes glittered. There was no doubting he appreciated this gift.

"You missed out a dark heart," Vance prompted me.

I was about to offer Jed up, for that had been my intention, when I heard a loud splash. Cold rancid pond water spattered me. Silvan waded up alongside me.

"Oh take mine," he said cheerfully.

"Silvan," I protested, but he waved me away.

"I'm as black as they come," he called up to Vance.

The ancient tree observed us with increasing interest. "So be it." Silvan nodded in contentment. "Now young Alfhild, that simply leaves a sacrifice of the living and the dead."

I glanced about at the witches who surrounded us. "I'm not sure about the dead," I said, feeling nervous at what was to come. "But for the living you can take me."

"Or me," offered Silvan and I looked at him in horror.

"Or me," said Jed quietly but firmly.

"Craaaaaarck!" said George.

"Hooo-oooo-oooo!" said Mr Hoo.

"Are you crazy?" I asked the owl, and he wobbled his head.

There was silence throughout the marsh as Vance considered all we'd offered him. It stretched on interminably. He gazed down at us, scrutinizing us all in turn and then looking at each of the witches who made up the Speckled Wood coven. I shivered in the cold water, partly from fear, but taking comfort in the security of Mr Hoo's feathers close to my cheek.

The sun's rays poked through the branches, low on the horizon, when finally Vance tipped back his mighty crown and began to shake. I started back, expecting his rage to fall upon us, but when I heard the bass tones of his booming laugh, I knew everything was going to be alright.

It turned out that Vance didn't really require any sort of sacrifice at all. We mollified him entirely by gifting him the Moridot. I handed it over, much to his delight, by pushing it into his trunk. It looked rather like a navel piercing.

But big enough for a tree.

It shimmered in the light as he shimmied proudly in the water.

"You're sure that's all you want?" I asked in confusion.

Vance leaned down to me, so that we were almost at eyelevel—he had to bend almost double, not easy for a tree of his size—and shook his branches. "You passed my exam with flying colours, Alf. I just wanted to test your mettle as the owner of Speckled Wood and the estate surrounding it. You have a brave true heart all of your own. You're compassionate and wise—for someone so young— and you pick your friends well."

I breathed in relief. "The sacrifices?" I asked.

"By all that's green! Great heavens, no thank you. Good magick does not profit from the misfortune of others. Be the good you want to see in the world, Alf."

"I'll try," I promised. I gestured around at the rank pool that surrounded him, and the drooping trees stretching far away in every direction. "And the water?"

"Give me some time," he said. "Everything gets better with time."

"Thank you, Vance," I said and hugged him, his bark rough and reassuringly solid beneath my cheek.

"Any time you want a chat, come and visit me," he instructed, and I promised I would.

As I started to walk away, he called after me. "You know, you're as talented a witch as your great grandmother. When I tested her many years ago, she was industrious and ingenious. You are her match."

That seemed high praise indeed to me, after all everyone was forever telling me what a brilliant witch Gwyn had been, and I have to admit I was buzzing with pride as I joined a group of my friends.

George sat on his rock croaking, and I half felt sorry for him.

Wizard Shadowmender and my father were just out of earshot at the edge of the woods, waiting to escort Jed to a secure location. I had no idea where that would be, but I doubted we would meet again. He met my eyes and we shared one last meaningful smile. There was no doubt that despite everything, Jed, now so accepting of his fate, had a brave heart too.

So it will probably come as no surprise when I confess... that my wand slipped in my hand.

"*Deformis bufo!*" I called, and in a silvery instant, Jed had shrunk.

I stared down at the hideously deformed monster toad I had created. "Wow—sorry about that. You are seriously ugly," I told him. Glancing back at the shocked faces of my father and Wizard Shadowmender I hurriedly pushed him towards George. "Now skedaddle you two!"

I watched in delight as they jumped together around the rocks, trusting that Vance would take good care of them for now, while I worked on forgiveness for them both.

And maybe sometime soon, when I felt mellow and kind, I'd come back for them.

EPiLOGUE

I awoke twenty-four hours later to the sound of bird song. Not of the volume I had grown used to during my residency at Whittle Inn, but an improvement on the deafening silence of the past few days.

Better than that, Mr Hoo had perched on the window settle. The sheen on his feathers was evident, where just twenty-four hours previously he had been dull and out of condition.

"Morning, little fella," I said and planted a kiss on his feathery head.

"Hooo-ooo," he said, and then twittered for a little while in excitement.

"Yes, I'm glad I didn't have to serve you up as an owly sacrifice too," I said, watching him perform a wobbly little dance.

I leaned out of the window to inhale the fresh

scent of the day. I thought I could smell rain in the air, but that was alright. I hoped it would rain heavily. It would help to flush the water table through. An IV drip for the countryside.

In the distance Speckled Wood stood taller and straighter than it had done yesterday—and I felt confident that Vance had already begun working his magick.

I stretched. "I'll have a shower and then I'd better help Charity with breakfast," I told Mr Hoo. And clean up after the fight. The bar and grounds, and the first floor—especially the landing outside my suite of rooms—had been left in a right state.

I spared a thought for George and Jed as I made myself ready to face the world, hoping they'd survived their first day and night in the wild unscathed.

"Because the goddess alone knows there's plenty of predators out there in the big wide world," I said, pulling on my robes and pocketing my wand, a new habit I intended to keep up.

As I stepped outside my room, Florence whizzed past me with her carpet sweeper. "Morning, Miss Alf," she sang. I smiled to see her so happy in her industry.

In the kitchen, Silvan looked up at me from his

newspaper as Monsieur Emietter plonked a plate of bacon and eggs in front of me.

"You're awake ridiculously early." I was amazed.

He shrugged. "You up for a spot of spellcasting practise later?"

"I assumed you'd be heading back to London now." I reached for the pepper. "We achieved what I asked you here for." To find George remained unspoken.

Silvan shrugged and returned to his paper. "I thought it might be fun to stick around for a bit."

"Oh," I said, munching thoughtfully on a piece of toast, wishing my vision could drill through the paper so I could read the expression on his face.

Zephaniah apparated into the kitchen, closely followed by Gwyn and Florence.

"Miss Alf," he said. "I think we may have an issue with some Japanese knotweed out the back."

Oh. It never rains but it pours. "What? No. Where's that come from? That stuff is deadly!"

"Never mind that," interrupted Gwyn. "What are you going to do about that hole in the cellar, Alf? We need to get it filled in as a matter of urgency."

Florence held up her feather duster. "Miss Alf? You'll never guess what I found in the Throne Room?"

Charity popped her head around the door. "Alf, I'm going to have to hire a plasterer. There are some huge holes in the walls upstairs."

Silvan dropped his paper an inch or two so that he could smirk at me, his dark eyes glittering in amusement.

I studied the travel company adverts on the back of *The Celestine Times*. "Sometimes, I think I'd just like to pack a bag and get away from it all," I said to him, as the voices of Gwyn, Charity and Zephaniah chimed in around me, the volume becoming progressively louder and their demands more vociferous.

Silvan nodded. "Maybe you should take a holiday."

"Maybe I should," I smiled thoughtfully.

WHERE NEXT FOR WONKY?

Find out, in *The Mysterious Mr Wylie: Wonky Book 6*

Dem bones, dem bones, dem dry bones ...

Building work at Whittle Inn has unearthed a skeleton.

Having recently returned from a holiday overseas, Alfhild Daemonne is horrified, but keen to find out who the unfortunate victim was and how they died. Could it have been witchcraft or some other dark magick? Or something more mundane?

What was the victim's link to Alf's wonky inn and why were they interred within the walls?

It soon becomes obvious that Alf isn't the only person who's interested in the discovery.

The mysterious Mr Wylie is paying a return visit to Whittlecombe, and it quickly transpires that nothing is as it initially appears.

Catch up on the latest chaotic adventures of your favourite witches, wizards, ghosts and villagers. And not forgetting Mr Hoo of course!

Pre-order Wonky Inn Book 6 on Amazon today. Release date: 30th April 2019

OUT NEXT FROM
JEANNIE WYCHERLEY

Midnight Garden

Lisa's mother is dying. But Lisa doesn't care...

Now in her early forties, and with her life disintegrating around her, she's been forced to return to her childhood home where the memories of her father and brother have long been repressed.

When the Victorian villa across the road goes up for sale, Lisa is naturally curious. One old woman has owned the property her whole life, and Lisa has never been allowed to step into the grounds before.

Now an odd young stranger invites her to explore the garden ... but only after midnight.

But as everyone knows, after midnight is when the nightmares really begin.

Soon Lisa will be all alone in the world, and that will suit her just fine. Won't it?

Not if her mother takes her guilty secret with her to the grave.

Lovers of contemporary gothic horror and dark fantasy will love this chilling little tale.

Midnight Garden (The Extra Ordinary World Novella Book 1) is available to pre-order on Amazon now.

PLEASE CONSIDER LEAVING A REVIEW?

If you have enjoyed reading *The Mystery of the Marsh Malaise*, please consider leaving me a review.

Reviews help to spread the word about my writing, which takes me a step closer to my dream of writing full time.

If you are kind enough to leave a review, please also consider joining my Author Street Team on Facebook – Jeannie Wycherley's Fiendish Street Team. Do let me know you left a review when you apply because it's a closed group. You can find my fiendish team here

You'll have the chance to Beta read and get your

hands-on advanced review eBook copies from time to time. I also appreciate your input when I need some help with covers, blurbs etc.

Or sign up for my newsletter here to keep up to date with what I'm doing next!

THE BIRTH OF WONKY

In Case You Missed

The story begins...

The Wonkiest Witch: Wonky Inn Book 1

Alfhild Daemonne has inherited an inn.
and a dead body.

Estranged from her witch mother, and having committed to little in her thirty years, Alf surprises herself when she decides to start a new life.

She heads deep into the English countryside intent on making a success of the once popular inn. However, discovering the murder throws her a curve ball. Especially when she suspects dark magick.

Additionally, a less than warm welcome from several locals, persuades her that a variety of folk – of both the mortal and magickal persuasions – have it in for her.

The dilapidated inn presents a huge challenge for Alf. Uncertain who to trust, she considers calling time on the venture.

Should she pack her bags and head back to London? Don't be daft.

Alf's magickal powers may be as wonky as the inn, but she's dead set on finding the murderer.

Once a witch always a witch, and this one is fighting back.

A clean and cozy witch mystery.

Take the opportunity to immerse yourself in this fantastic new witch mystery series, from the author of the award-winning novel, Crone.

Grab Book 1 of the Wonky Inn series, The Wonkiest Witch, on Amazon now.

The Mysterious Mr Wylie: Wonky Inn Book 6

The Witch Who Killed Christmas: Wonky Inn Christmas Special

ALSO BY

Beyond the Veil (2018)

Crone (2017)

A Concerto for the Dead and Dying (short story, 2018)

Deadly Encounters: A collection of short stories (2017)

Keepers of the Flame: A love story (Novella, 2018)

Non Fiction

Losing my best Friend Thoughtful support for those
affected by dog bereavement or pet loss (2017)

Follow Jeannie Wycherley

Find out more at on the website www.jeanniewycherley.
co.uk

You can tweet Jeannie twitter.com/Thecushionlady

Or visit her on Facebook for her fiction www.

facebook.com/jeanniewycherley

Sign up for Jeannie's newsletter http://
eepurl.com/cN3Q6L

Coming Soon

Coming Summer 2019

The Municipality of Lost Souls by Jeannie Wycherley
Described as a cross between Daphne Du Maurier's *Jamaica Inn*, and TV's *The Walking Dead*, but with ghosts instead of zombies, *The Municipality of Lost Souls* tells the story of Amelia Fliss and her cousin Agatha Wick.

In the otherwise quiet municipality of Durscombe, the inhabitants of the small seaside town harbour a deadly secret.

Amelia Fliss, wife of a wealthy merchant, is the lone voice who speaks out against the deadly practice of

the wrecking and plundering of ships on the rocks in
Lyme bay, but no-one appears to be listening to her.
As evil and malcontent spread like cholera
throughout the community, and the locals point
fingers and vow to take vengeance against outsiders,
the dead take it upon themselves to end a barbaric
tradition the living seem to lack the will to stop.

Set in Devon in the UK during the 1860s, *The
Municipality of Lost Souls* is a Victorian Gothic
ghost story, with characters who will leave their mark
on you forever.

If you enjoyed *Crone* or *Beyond the Veil*, you really
don't want to miss this novel.

Sign up for my newsletter or join my Facebook group
today.

Printed in Poland
by Amazon Fulfillment
Poland Sp. z o.o., Wrocław

54754725R00188